Lost in her stars

FAHED ABDULLAH

BlueRose ONE .com
Stories Matter
NewDelhi • London

BLUEROSE PUBLISHERS
India | U.K.

BlueRose ONE.com
Stories Matter
NewDelhi • London

For permissions requests or inquiries regarding this publication, please contact:

BLUEROSE PUBLISHERS
www.BlueRoseONE.com
info@bluerosepublishers.com
+91 8882 898 898
+4407342408967

ISBN: 978-93-7018-285-1

Cover design: Yash Singhal
Typesetting: Namrata Saini

First Edition: January 2026

Chapter-1

This is the story of an ordinary boy and an extraordinary girl. It's not a mystery that can't be easily unraveled, but rather a depth that must be felt....a blend of pain, joy, and those priceless moments that color life in its truest hues. So, brace yourself, for this is no ordinary tale. It's a story of something hidden deep within the heart, something that goes beyond what words can convey.

Like any story worth telling, it begins with a girl. My name is Fawaz, and I'm 21 years old. Like many young men from well-off families, I've had a comfortable life, complete with a loving home and a caring family. I was born on October 12th, 1999, and have a younger sister, Ayesha. She's the real charm of our family, always bringing light to our home in Ranchi.

From a young age, I dreamed of becoming an engineer. That dream led me to one of the toughest entrance exams in India, the JEE. Although my score wasn't exceptional, it was enough to secure me a place at KIIT in Bhubaneswar. Soon after the results were announced, I packed my bags and prepared to start this new chapter of my life. Up until that point, everything had been normal....perfect, even from my perspective.

As the day of my departure approached, I was ready to embark on my journey to Bhubaneswar. It was an eight-hour drive from Ranchi, and as I sat in the car, staring out the window, I couldn't help but reflect on everything I was leaving behind.

The sky that day was clearer than I'd ever seen it, stretching endlessly above me. Memories flooded my mind…happy moments spent with family and friends, and a small wave of sadness washed over me as I realized that I was leaving that familiar world behind. I couldn't help but wonder what this new life had in store for me.

Chapter-2

After unpacking my things in the cozy hostel room—two beds, two study tables, and a window that framed a view of the campus perfectly—I decided I needed a break. The room had everything I needed to start this new chapter, but I felt restless. I grabbed my phone and headed out, thinking a quick walk would help me clear my head.

As I wandered through the campus, I found myself drawn to the central courtyard, where students were lounging around, chatting, and soaking up the sun. That's when I saw her.

She stood out in the crowd like a lighthouse in the fog, effortlessly drawing my attention. Her beauty was the kind that wasn't just about looks—it was in the way she carried herself, with a grace that made everything around her seem a little more vibrant. Her deep, sparkling blue eyes caught mine for a fleeting moment, and I felt an inexplicable connection, like the universe had just paused for that one heartbeat. Her long, flowing brown hair swayed gently with the breeze, and I could barely tear my eyes away as she continued on her way, unaware of the impact she'd just had on me.

I'm still thinking about her, so I made my way back to the hostel. The image of her stayed with me, but I knew I'd likely never see her again. Life had a way of moving on, even when you wanted to hold onto a moment.

I was still lost in thought when I reached my room, only to find someone already there. Somebody about my age, with a broad smile and a confident stance, was just finishing up unpacking his bags.

"Hey, you must be Fawaz," he said, noticing me at the door.

"Yeah, that's me. And you?" I replied, stepping inside.

"Aryan," he said, extending a hand. "Looks like we're roommates."

We shook hands, and I noticed the gym bag on his bed. Aryan was clearly into fitness—his toned arms and broad shoulders were a dead giveaway. As we got talking, I found out he was from Rewa, a city in Madhya Pradesh, and he had a knack for bringing people together. He handed me a piece of homemade kalakand, and I couldn't help but smile at the gesture.

Aryan was the kind of guy who made everything seem easy. He had a natural charm and an effortless style that made him stand out, but it was his down-to-earth attitude that really clicked with me. As we continued to chat, I found myself easing into the idea of sharing this space with him. We both discovered we were in the same section—A6 for Computer Science—and it felt like another sign that this was going to be a great friendship.

As I lay in bed that night, thoughts of the girl I'd seen and the new roommate I'd met swirled in my mind. I had a feeling that life was about to get a lot more interesting.

Chapter-3

We entered our classroom for the first time, feeling a mix of excitement and curiosity. The room was pristine, with neatly arranged desks and a warm, welcoming atmosphere. Aryan and I chose the fifth bench in the second row, dropping our bags as we exchanged a quick glance that said, "This is it."

After taking a brief stroll around the campus, soaking in the newness of everything, we returned to our seats, ready to dive into the day. Just as we were getting comfortable, a boy and a girl walked in together. There was something about the way they moved, in sync, like they had known each other forever. They took their seats right in front of us on the fourth bench.

The boy turned around, a friendly smile on his face. "Hey, I'm Siddhart," he said, extending his hand. "And this is Riya."

Aryan and I introduced ourselves, shaking hands with them. It was a simple exchange, but there was an ease to it, as if we'd known each other for a while.

"You guys from around here?" Aryan asked.

Siddhart chuckled. "Nah, we're both from New Delhi. We had k nown each other since we were kids, actually."

Riya nodded, adding with a smile, "Our families have been close for generations. It's nice to have someone familiar around."

We all exchanged a few more words, the conversation flowing naturally, and I couldn't help but notice how comfortable they seemed with each other. It was clear they had each other's backs, a bond that had been formed long before college began.

As I was getting my things in order, making sure my notebooks and pens were neatly arranged, Riya suddenly leaned over, her curiosity piqued. "Hey, do you always keep things organized ?" she asked, a playful glint in her eye.

I looked up, slightly surprised. "Yeah, I guess I like to keep things in order. Makes life easier, you know?"

Before I could say anything more, Siddhart jumped in, teasing Riya. "And here I thought you were the organized one," he said, nudging her lightly.

Riya shot him a mock glare. "Oh, please. You know I'm the one who keeps you from losing your head!"

Their banter quickly escalated, and what started as a light-hearted exchange turned into a full-blown mock argument. Aryan and I couldn't help but chuckle as they went back and forth, their chemistry unmistakable.

At one point, Riya turned to us with an exaggerated sigh. "See what I have to deal with? And you guys are just laughing!"

Siddhart, pretending to be wounded, asked, "Wait, how did this become my fault?"

I decided to step in, grinning as I said, "Alright, alright, let's call it a draw. No need to start a rivalry on day one."

Aryan, always quick with a joke, added, "You two are like an old married couple. We're going to have our hands full with you."

Just as the laughter settled, the door creaked open, and in walked a boy who seemed to carry the weight of the world on his shoulders—Azal. His eyes held a quiet intensity. With him was his twin brother, Abad, whose presence was a stark contrast. Abad had the kind of charisma that could make anyone feel at ease, and it wasn't long before he was chatting away with us like we'd known each other for years.

Abad wasn't just any student, though—he was a professional cricketer. His name was already well-known in sports circles, and his easy-going demeanor made it hard to imagine him under pressure on the field. But there was no mistaking the drive in his eyes, the kind that only comes from chasing a dream with everything you've got.

Not long after, a girl with a bright, infectious smile—Preeti—joined us, her laughter instantly filling the room. The energy in the room was vibrant, and I could feel that this group was something special.

Then, just when I thought the day couldn't get any more interesting, she walked in—the girl I'd seen earlier. My heart skipped a beat as she entered the room, her presence commanding my full attention. Aryan, ever observant, gave me a knowing look and a pat on the back. "Looks like your day just got better," he whispered.

She made her way over to Preeti, her eyes lighting up with recognition. "Hi, I'm Zoya Himani," she introduced herself, her voice soft yet clear, like a melody that lingered in the air.

As she spoke, I couldn't help but feel like everything else had faded into the background. Zoya. Her name suited her perfectly—delicate yet strong.

In just twenty minutes, I'd met some of the most intriguing people I could have hoped for, but it was Zoya who left the strongest impression. That night, as I told my family about my new friends—my entire gang—I couldn't help but linger on the memory of Zoya. Later, as I opened a new diary to record the details of this unforgettable day, I realized just how lucky I was to have met her.

Chapter-4

The next evening, after our last class of the day, our gang decided to meet at KIIT Square. It was a lively spot on campus, perfect for hanging out and unwinding.

Aryan and I were buzzing with excitement as we headed out, eager to enjoy the evening. We agreed to meet the others near Burger King.

At the girls' hostel, Preeti and Zoya were debating whether to join us. Zoya was still hesitant.

"Come on, Zoya, it's our first day! Let's not waste it," Preeti urged.

"I don't want to be the odd one out, but I'm not sure," Zoya replied.

Preeti managed to convince her, and soon they joined us at KIIT Square. I was immediately struck by how stunning Zoya looked in her knee-length skirt and top. Her presence was captivating, and I could hardly take my eyes off her.

As we gathered near Burger King, the conversation began to flow naturally. Aryan and I were chatting with Siddhart about our plans for the weekend.

"I've been meaning to ask you, Siddhart, what are you into?" I asked, curious about his interests.

Siddhart shrugged. "Honestly, I'm more into dancing and music than sports. What about you, Abad?"

Meanwhile, Abad, who had been quietly observing the conversation, decided to answer Sid. "Actually, I've been pretty immersed in cricket for the past few years."

"Cricket? That's cool!" Siddhart responded. "What's your journey been like?"

Abad took a deep breath. "Well, it's been quite a ride. I've been playing professionally for a while now. It's been rewarding, but also tough. Especially recently."

Siddhart raised an eyebrow. "Tough? How so?"

Abad looked down, struggling with his emotions. "It's not just the game itself. There's been a lot of personal stuff happening. My twin brother Azal went through something really rough."

Azal, who had been quietly smoking a cigarette, finally spoke up. "Manisha and I were in love, but our families couldn't accept our relationship. She was Hindu, and I'm Muslim. The pressure was too much, and we broke up. I still love her, but we lost each other."

The group fell silent, absorbing the weight of Azal's words. Zoya's eyes filled with tears as she listened, her empathy clear.

"Azal, I'm so sorry," Zoya said softly. "That must have been incredibly painful."

Abad nodded, his voice filled with compassion. "We're all here for you, Azal. It's okay to feel this way, and you don't have to go through it alone."

Siddhart, moved by the situation, added, “I didn’t know about all this. It’s really tough, but you have friends here who care about you.”

I took a moment to lighten the mood a bit. “Azal, you’re always the best dressed—clearly winning the style game tonight, by the way.” I teased, trying to bring some levity.

He laughed, and Zoya’s smile returned. I couldn’t help but notice how her presence made everything seem a little brighter.

As the evening drew to a close, we shared a quiet moment, appreciating the strength of our bond and the importance of being there for one another. My heart was not beating dub-dub….it was luv-luv, but this time, it was a love grounded in understanding and shared experiences.

Chapter-5

The college was abuzz with excitement as the annual Cultural Festival approached. Posters and decorations adorned every corner of the campus, and students were eagerly preparing for the big day. This year, the festival was themed around traditional cultures, and everyone was encouraged to dress in their finest traditional attire.

Aryan and I decided to embrace the theme fully. We donned vibrant kurtas—mine in a rich royal blue and Aryan's in a striking maroon. The intricate embroidery added a touch of elegance, and we paired our outfits with matching churidar pants and stylish *mojris.*

At the girls' hostel, Preeti, Zoya, and Riya were busy preparing for the festival. They emerged in stunning lehengas—Preeti in a deep red lehenga with gold accents, Zoya in a beautiful green lehenga with delicate embroidery, and Riya in a vibrant blue lehenga with intricate patterns. Their hair was styled in traditional updos, adorned with jasmine flowers.

When we met at the festival grounds, the sight was truly breathtaking. The entire campus had been transformed into a vibrant celebration of culture. Colorful stalls lined the paths, each showcasing a different aspect of traditional art, crafts, and food. Music played softly in the background, blending traditional melodies with contemporary rhythms.

Abad joined us, looking distinguished in a cream kurta with a matching vest. Siddhart, who had chosen a subtle yet sophisticated beige kurta, and Azal, dressed in a stylish kurta, were also part of the group.

"Wow, everyone looks amazing!" I said, admiring their attire. "This festival is turning out to be incredible."

Aryan nodded in agreement. "Definitely. The energy here is fantastic."

We walked through the festival, stopping at various stalls, sampling traditional foods and exploring the crafts. There was intricate hand-painted pottery, beautiful textiles, and a stall where you could get henna designs. The aromas of spicy curries and sweet desserts filled the air.

We came across a stage where traditional dance performances were taking place. Zoya, Preeti, and Riya were mesmerized by a Bharatanatyam performance, their eyes following every graceful movement. Azal, who had been quiet lately, seemed to find solace in the lively atmosphere.

"I've been waiting for this," Azal said, sampling a plate of chaat. "The food here is incredible."

"Yeah, the chaat is fantastic," Abad agreed, grabbing a bite. "This place really knows how to throw a festival."

Siddhart grinned as he tried a sweet from one of the stalls. "I think I'm going to need a few more of these."

As the evening progressed, we all gathered around an ice cream stall, enjoying the cool treat and the lively conversation. Aryan, Siddhart, and Abad shared light-hearted stories and playful banter about past festivals and family traditions.

Preeti nudged Zoya with a playful grin. "You know, Zoya, I think someone's been caught staring at you all evening."

Zoya's eyes widened slightly as she glanced at me. There was a brief moment of hesitation before she looked away. "Really? And who might that be?"

"Oh, I think you know exactly who," Preeti teased, glancing over at me with a knowing smile.

I felt my face heat up as Zoya's gaze met mine again. "Caught red-handed, I guess," I said with a sheepish smile.

Zoya's smile was hesitant, and she looked away quickly, her cheeks flushing slightly. "Oh… well, I didn't realize."

Riya, who had been listening to the conversation, joined in with a teasing tone. "Looks like someone's got a bit of a crush."

I tried to play it cool. "Hey, it's not my fault if someone catches my eye."

Later in the evening, as we continued to enjoy our ice cream, Riya and Preeti pulled me aside. "We need to talk," Riya said, her tone a mix of concern and curiosity.

Preeti nodded. "Yeah, you've been pretty obvious about your feelings for Zoya. It's clear you like her."

I felt my heart race. "Oh? And what about it?"

Riya gave me a serious look. "It's not just that. Zoya seems a bit… hesitant. We noticed her reaction earlier."

Preeti added, "She likes you, but there's something holding her back. She mentioned she can't start something right now. We don't know the details, but it's important to understand her situation."

I nodded, feeling a mix of concern and determination. “Thanks for the heads-up. I’ll try to respect her feelings and wait for her to open up.”

As the evening drew to a close, we all got tired and went to our respective hostels.

Chapter-6

The evening was winding down, and the quiet of the night settled over the campus. Aryan, Siddhart, Abad, Azal, and I had gathered on my balcony, enjoying the cool breeze and the peaceful view of the campus lights.

Azal, who had been quite subdued lately, pulled out a pack of cigarettes. "Anyone up for learning how to smoke?" he asked, a hint of a smile on his face.

Aryan, Siddhart, and I exchanged glances. "Sure, why not?" I said, trying to sound casual. It seemed like a typical boys' moment, and we were all curious.

Azal demonstrated how to light a cigarette and take a drag. He passed the pack around, and we each took turns, following his instructions. The taste was harsh, but there was something strangely satisfying about it.

As we relaxed and shared some laughs, I found myself opening up about my feelings for Zoya. "You guys, I can't stop thinking about Zoya. She's just so beautiful, and the way she smiles… it's like she lights up the room."

Aryan nodded in agreement. "I've noticed that too. There's something about her that's really captivating."

Siddhart chuckled. "Man, you're really head over heels, aren't you?"

I grinned. "Yeah, I guess I am. There's just something about her that feels special."

Azal took a deep drag from his cigarette, exhaling slowly. "Love is a beautiful thing," he said softly. "But you've got to be careful. It doesn't always go the way you want it to."

The mood shifted as Azal continued, his voice growing more serious. "I had someone special... Manisha. We were deeply in love, but her family didn't accept our relationship. It was devastating for her, and it was tough for me too. I still care for her, but it didn't turn out the way I hoped."

Siddhart and Aryan listened intently, their expressions somber. "It's tough when love doesn't work out," Siddhart said quietly. "Especially when there's so much more to it than just feelings."

Azal nodded, a pained expression on his face. "She was the most amazing person, and losing her was like losing a part of myself. Even though it was hard for both of us, it was particularly challenging for her."

The group fell silent for a moment, absorbing the gravity of Azal's words. The air was filled with a mixture of reflection and understanding. It was clear that Azal's experience had left a mark on him, and we all felt a deeper connection with him at that moment.

Aryan broke the silence with a supportive tone. "We're here for you, man. It's important to talk about these things, and it's clear that you're still carrying a lot with you."

Azal nodded appreciatively. "Thanks. It helps to have friends who understand."

As the night continued, our conversation turned to lighter topics, but the weight of Azal's story lingered with us. We shared more laughs and stories, and the camaraderie between us felt stronger than ever.

As we finally wrapped up the night, we headed back to our respective rooms.

Chapter-7

After a few days had passed, we finally got a 5-day holiday due to some local festivals and the arrival of second-year students in the college. The morning sun bathed the campus in a warm glow as we prepared for our much-anticipated trip to Barunei Hills. The idea had been floated casually the week before, but now, with everyone excitedly packing bags and chatting animatedly, it felt like an adventure was truly underway.

We had rented a van, and the energy was electric as we loaded our gear and settled into our seats. Aryan was at the wheel, his enthusiasm evident as he navigated us out of the campus and onto the highway. Siddhart was in charge of the music, curating a playlist that ranged from classic rock to the latest hits. The rest of us were scattered around, engaging in lively conversation.

As we drove, the landscape gradually changed from the urban sprawl of Bhubaneswar to the lush, rolling hills that marked our destination. The anticipation was palpable, and I could feel my excitement building with each passing kilometer.

"Are we there yet?" Preeti asked playfully from the back seat, her voice a mix of impatience and amusement.

"Almost!" Aryan called back, glancing at the road. "Just a little further."

Zoya, sitting beside me, was quietly enjoying the view. Her presence beside me felt both comforting and nerve-wracking. I had been wrestling with the idea of confessing my feelings to her during this trip, but every time I considered it, doubts clouded my mind.

Finally, we arrived at Barunei Hills. The van parked at the base, and we were greeted by the cool, fresh air and the breathtaking view of the rolling green hills. The path to the top was a winding trail, and as we began our ascent, the laughter and chatter of the group filled the air.

The hike was invigorating, with each step revealing more of the stunning landscape around us. We stopped frequently to take photos, share snacks, and enjoy the beauty of nature. At one point, Abad and Siddhart challenged each other to a race, much to everyone's amusement. Preeti and Zoya were engrossed in a conversation about their favorite books, while Aryan and I lagged behind, discussing our plans for the upcoming semester.

Eventually, we reached a scenic viewpoint that offered a panoramic view of the surrounding hills. We spread out on the grass, soaking in the view and catching our breath.

"This place is amazing," Aryan said, stretching out on the grass. "Totally worth the hike."

"Definitely," I agreed, trying to push aside my nerves. This was the moment I had been waiting for, but my heart raced as I prepared myself for what I was about to say.

As the sun began its descent, casting a golden hue over the hills, I took a deep breath and approached Zoya, who was sitting alone, taking in the view. My heart pounded as I sat down beside her.

"Zoya," I began, trying to keep my voice steady. "There's something I've been meaning to tell you."

She turned to me, her eyes reflecting the warmth of the setting sun. "What is it, Fawaz?"

I hesitated, searching for the right words. "I've been thinking about us. I really like you, Zoya. I feel something special between us, and I want to see where this could go."

For a moment, there was a silence that felt like an eternity. Zoya's expression was one of contemplation, and I could see the conflict in her eyes.

"Fawaz," she finally said softly, "I... I appreciate your feelings. I really do. But I don't think I can be what you're looking for."

My heart sank. "Why not? Is it something I did?"

"No," she replied quickly. "It's not about you. It's just... My life is complicated. There are things I'm dealing with that I can't drag you into. It's best for you if you don't get involved with me."

Her words hit me like a blow. I struggled to process what she was saying. "But why? What's so complicated that it would make it impossible for us?"

Zoya looked away, her gaze lost in the horizon. "It's not something I can explain easily. It's about my family. There are aspects of my life that would only bring you trouble, and I don't want that for you. You deserve someone who can give you what you need without all this... baggage."

The pain in her words was clear, and I felt a mixture of confusion and frustration. "I don't care about the baggage, Zoya.

I care about you. I just don't understand why you're pushing me away."

Before she could respond, the rest of the group started gathering around, sensing that something was off. Preeti, noticing the tension, approached with a concerned look. "Everything okay, you two?"

Zoya quickly composed herself, forcing a smile. "Yes, we just needed a moment to ourselves."

The group continued to mingle, but the mood had shifted. I could see the concern in my friends' eyes as they glanced between Zoya and me, but they respected our privacy.

As the evening progressed, the once joyful atmosphere felt heavier. Zoya remained quiet, and I struggled to maintain my composure. The conversations around me were a blur as I tried to make sense of what had just happened.

Later, as we made our way back down the trail, I stayed towards the back, reflecting on Zoya's words. Despite the heartbreak, I appreciated her honesty, even if it didn't make the situation any easier.

Back at the van, the drive home was subdued. The vibrant energy from earlier was replaced by a quiet reflection. I sat beside Zoya, our conversation limited to polite small talk, but the connection we had once shared felt distant.

As we returned to campus, the once exciting trip had left me with a mix of emotions—confusion, sadness, and a lingering sense of longing. I knew this experience would be a pivotal moment for me and for Zoya, but only time would reveal what the future held.

The night ended with everyone heading to their respective rooms, and I was left alone with my thoughts. My heart was heavy, and the echoes of Zoya's words replayed in my mind. As I lay in bed, I couldn't shake the feeling that this was just the beginning of a more complex journey for both of us.

Chapter-8

The next day, I found myself sitting in class, my attention fixated on Zoya. Her presence seemed to fill the room, every glance of her milky white cheeks, tinged with a gentle blush, and the cascade of her thick, brown hair that shone with a radiance surpassing the sun. My heart raced as I tried to concentrate on the lecture, but my thoughts kept drifting back to her.

I tried to focus on the professor's words, but the sight of Zoya's serene face and the way her hair fell around her shoulders made it nearly impossible. I was madly in love, obsessing over her every gesture, her every smile. Despite my attempts to stay composed, I couldn't help but be drawn to her, feeling like I was under some spell.

After the lecture, I decided to take a chance. With a nervous yet determined breath, I approached her as we transitioned between classes. "Zoya, do you want to grab a milkshake after class?" I asked, trying to keep my voice steady.

Her eyes widened in surprise, and for a moment, I feared she might decline. But then she smiled softly. "Sure, I'd like that."

I couldn't believe my luck. As soon as the class ended, our friends—Aryan, Siddhart, Riya, Preeti, Abad, and Azal—left us alone, sensing the importance of this moment. Zoya, noticing their departure, cast a playful frown in their direction. "I can't believe they just left us like that," she said with a hint of annoyance.

We walked to the nearby cafe and picked up our milkshakes, the cool sweetness of the drinks a refreshing contrast to the nervous flutter in my chest. We made our way to the MBA Garden, a tranquil spot on campus that looked stunning in the evening light.

The garden was a haven of peace, with lush greenery and neatly manicured paths. The evening sky was a canvas of deepening blues and twinkling stars, a rare sight amidst the urban haze.

We found a quiet spot on a bench under a canopy of trees. I took a deep breath, trying to gather my thoughts. "Zoya, I've been meaning to ask you… about the other day. You mentioned something about family. What's going on?"

She hesitated, taking a sip of her milkshake as she avoided eye contact. "It's... complicated. It's not something I can easily explain."

I could sense her reluctance, and it only heightened the tension between us. "Is it really that complicated? Can't we talk about it?"

I tried to press further, but she shifted the conversation. "Look at the sky tonight. It's clearer than usual. Pollution makes it so hard to see the stars."

I glanced up, taking in the sight of the starlit sky. "Yes, it is clearer tonight. The stars are beautiful."

Zoya continued, her gaze fixed on the moon. "And the moon… it looks so beautiful tonight."

I couldn't resist the urge to compliment her. "Just like you," I said, trying to keep my tone light yet sincere.

She blushed, her cheeks turning a shade of pink that matched the evening sky. But then she shook her head, trying to refocus. "Enough about the sky. I've been struggling with calculus. Could you help me out?"

I was taken aback by her sudden change in subject but gladly accepted. "Of course, I'd be happy to help. Let's go over it together."

We spent the next hour working through calculus problems, the atmosphere relaxed and comfortable. Zoya's initial hesitation faded as she showed genuine interest and appreciation for my help. In her heart, I sensed she was also holding onto feelings, but she kept them suppressed, hidden behind her calm exterior.

As the evening wound down, we walked back to our hostels, the cool night air a pleasant contrast to the warmth of our earlier interaction. At the hostel, Riya and Preeti were waiting for Zoya, their eyes sparkling with mischief.

"Look who finally showed up!" Preeti teased, her grin widening. "How was your evening with Fawaz?"

Zoya's face flushed with a deep blush, and she avoided their gaze. "It was… nice," she replied, her voice barely above a whisper.

Riya nudged her playfully. "Oh, come on! You two seemed to have a great time. You're blushing like a tomato!"

Preeti joined in, "Fawaz is a really good guy. Maybe you should give him a chance. Don't be so stubborn."

Zoya sighed, looking conflicted. "It's not that simple. There are things I can't just ignore."

Riya and Preeti exchanged glances, sensing her hesitation. "Just think about it, okay? Sometimes you need to take a leap of faith," Preeti said gently.

Despite their encouragement, Zoya remained hesitant. She appreciated their concern but knew there were complexities she couldn't easily resolve. As the teasing subsided, she retired to her room, her mind a swirl of emotions and thoughts.

The night ended with me feeling a mix of hope and uncertainty, eager to understand Zoya's feelings but unsure of what lay ahead. My heart was full of longing, but her answer left me with more questions than answers.

Chapter-9

The Sunday sun was bright as ever, and the college cricket ground buzzed with excitement. Our class had set up a match against the third-year students, and anticipation hung in the air like the scent of freshly cut grass. Abad, our captain and wicket-keeper, was the focal point of our team. Inspired by MS Dhoni, though he played as a leftie.

As the match commenced, the atmosphere crackled with energy. Abad and Karun took to the field as the opening batsmen. Abad, with his trademark composure, quickly established dominance. His shots were precise and elegant, and before long, he reached a half-century. The crowd, including Preeti, Zoya, Riya, and several other girls, cheered enthusiastically. I managed to contribute as well, hitting a few boundaries that brought our team to a respectable score.

The excitement didn't end with our innings. One of the girls from our class…Sneha, visibly impressed by Abad's performance, approached him after the match. Her cheeks flushed as she asked him out on a date. Abad, initially caught off guard, blushed deeply but accepted with a shy smile. The cheer from our friends was thunderous, and it seemed like a perfect end to our innings.

However, the mood took a sharp turn as the second innings began. The tension in the air was palpable, and the game soon descended into chaos. Siddhart, frustrated with a disputed run count, found himself in a heated argument with Rohit, a senior player. Rohit, losing his temper, slapped Siddhart across the face. The sting of the slap and Siddhart's shocked expression ignited a fierce surge of anger in me. Without thinking, I charged at Rohit, landing a punch that sent him staggering.

Rohit, enraged, shoved me violently. Dust and debris flew as the fight escalated. Aryan joined in, and soon it was a full-blown fight, with fists flying and shouts echoing across the field. The fight was chaotic and brutal, with both sides clashing in a whirlwind of violence. The seniors, initially taken aback, soon rallied and countered our aggression.

In the midst of the chaos, Zoya stood frozen, her eyes wide with terror. Her fear was palpable, and it struck me like a physical blow. The sight of her, unable to move and overwhelmed by the violence, made me realize the gravity of the situation. Her face, usually so calm and composed, was now a mask of pure panic.

Finally, the fight was broken up by a group of students from both sides. The atmosphere was charged with tension as we were warned about our conduct with seniors. I emerged from the brawl with a bloody elbow, a swollen eye, and a bruised ego. The adrenaline that had fueled the fight was now replaced by a throbbing pain and a deep sense of regret.

As we regrouped, Zoya, Siddhart, Riya, Preeti, Azal, Abad, and Sneha gathered together. The girls, particularly Zoya, took on the role of caretakers. We moved to a quieter spot near the canteen. Zoya's expression was a blend of worry and determination as she began to tend to my injuries.

As the evening progressed, the others went their separate ways. Abad and Sneha canceled their date and went to purchase antiseptic cream for all of us. Siddhart and Riya went to hang out, Azal went to buy cigarettes, and Aryan went to the gym. Nothing could keep him out of the gym. This left Zoya and me alone, the quiet of the canteen area contrasting sharply with the earlier chaos.

Her hands, though gentle, were firm as she cleaned my swollen eye with warm water. The pain from the fight was intense, but Zoya's touch was soothing. Her focus was entirely on me, and the contrast between her caring demeanor and the violence of the fight was striking. Each touch was a reminder of her concern, and I felt a deep sense of vulnerability.

As Zoya worked on my injuries, her gaze occasionally met mine. Her eyes were soft, filled with a mixture of affection and worry. The silence between us was charged with unspoken emotions. I found myself lost in thoughts of a future where moments like these were a regular part of our lives. The thought of being with her, sharing both the good times and the challenging ones, felt like a distant but desirable dream.

Suddenly, Zoya's hand landed gently but firmly on my shoulder. Her voice, though soft, carried a note of sternness. "No more fighting," she said, her eyes locking onto mine with a blend of concern and affection. "I don't want you to get hurt again."

Her words were a shock to my system. The intensity of her concern hit me hard. I had been so focused on the fight, on defending my friends, that I hadn't considered how my actions might affect those I cared about. The realization that Zoya was deeply affected by the violence was both humbling and heartwarming.

I nodded, feeling a surge of gratitude and a newfound resolve. "I promise," I said, my voice sincere. Her smile, despite the worry in her eyes, was a beacon of warmth and reassurance.

Zoya continued to treat my injuries with meticulous care. Her movements were gentle, her touch soothing. The soft glow of the evening light cast a warm hue over us, and the campus around us seemed to fade into the background. I sat there, feeling a profound sense of connection and tenderness. The earlier fight seemed distant, replaced by the intimacy of this moment.

As Zoya finished treating my swollen eye, she looked at me with a mixture of relief and affection. The silence between us was filled with unspoken emotions. I could see the affection she had for me, though she tried to keep it suppressed. Her concern, her gentle touch, and her caring nature spoke volumes.

In that moment, I felt a deep sense of gratitude and hope. Zoya's presence made me feel valued and cared for, and I knew that despite the chaos of the day, something beautiful had emerged from it.

Chapter-10

The cricket match against the third-year students had been more intense than any of us anticipated. The game had started as a friendly competition, but by the end, it was a battlefield. The bruises on our bodies were only a fraction of the pain we felt.

The morning sun filtered through the hostel windows, casting a gentle glow on the bruised faces of Abad, Azal, Siddhart, Aryan, and me. The remnants of yesterday's battle were evident in every painful movement and groan. Abad was still waking up, his left hand cradling his bruised ribs, while Siddhart was nursing a black eye that seemed to have a life of its own.

By midday, the campus was abuzz with gossip about the fight. Despite the pain, we had to go through our routine. The occasional glance or whisper from classmates was a reminder of the chaotic scene we had been part of.

Sneha found Abad in the mess hall. She was gentle as she approached him, her eyes full of concern. "Abad, how are you holding up?"

Abad smiled through the pain. "I'm okay, Sncha. Just a bit sore."

Sneha sat beside him, her gaze lingering on him longer than necessary. "You were incredible out there. I mean, the way you played… it was something."

Abad's cheeks flushed slightly. "Thanks, Sneha. I didn't expect to impress anyone, let alone someone like you."

As they talked, there was an undeniable spark between them. Sneha's eyes sparkled with admiration, and Abad's usual confidence seemed to be overshadowed by something more genuine.

Back at the hostel, the mood was a mix of pain and camaraderie. Riya and Preeti were busy tending to our injuries, their hands deftly working on the cuts and bruises. Despite the hurt, their presence was a comfort.

Riya looked at Siddhart's swollen eyes and sighed. "You really took one for the team, didn't you?"

Siddhart managed a weak smile. "Had to. Nobody messes with my friends."

Preeti, working on my elbow, added, "You all were so brave. But next time, maybe try to avoid fights that get this messy."

Zoya arrived with a concerned expression, her eyes scanning the room. "How's everyone doing?" she asked quietly.

I caught her gaze and saw the worry in her eyes. "We're managing, thanks to everyone's help."

Zoya nodded, though her face betrayed a deeper worry. "I'm glad you're all okay."

Later, Zoya and I found ourselves alone in the canteen area. She was gently cleaning my black eye, her touch surprisingly soothing despite the circumstances. I was acutely aware of her closeness, her soft hands on my skin, and the warmth radiating from her.

As she worked, she suddenly paused, her eyes meeting mine. "Why did you have to fight like that? You could've been seriously hurt."

I looked at her, the seriousness of her concern touching me deeply. "I couldn't just stand by and let him hurt Siddhart. It's not in me."

Zoya's eyes softened, and she let out a small sigh. "I understand, but please, no more fighting. I don't want to see you get hurt again."

I nodded, feeling a rush of gratitude and affection. "I promise."

As the evening rolled in, Abad and Sneha left for their date. Abad, despite his injuries, had an uncharacteristic bounce in his step, clearly excited about spending time with Sneha. They walked away together, deep in conversation, their chemistry undeniable.

Azal, who had been observing from a distance, approached me with a concerned look. "You know, Abad's really into Sneha. I hope this doesn't complicate things."

I nodded. "I think they have something special. It's good for him."

Azal's expression remained serious. "I just hope it doesn't lead to more trouble, especially with everything else going on."

As night fell, Zoya and I were talking on the phone, her thoughts seemingly far away. I could feel her with me, my heart aching with a mixture of longing and concern. Despite the pain, there was a strange comfort in the quiet moments we shared. I could sense the weight of her own troubles, though she never spoke of them.

"Take care of yourself, okay?" She said to me,

I nodded, my heart swelling with emotion. "I will. Thanks for everything."

Zoya's smile widened slightly, though it was tinged with sadness. "Just remember, I'm here if you need me."

As we cut the call, I sat alone, reflecting on the day's events. The bruises would heal, but the emotions and connections forged in the midst of chaos would linger. The night was quiet, but the echoes of the day's struggles and the budding relationships were far from silent.

Chapter-11

After their date, Abad was walking back to his hostel, his mind swirling with thoughts of Sneha. He couldn't shake the feeling of happiness, but it was mixed with a growing concern about the future. The differences between them—particularly their religions—are hard to ignore. As he approached his room, he found Azal waiting for him outside, leaning against the wall with a serious expression.

Azal said to him. "We need to talk, brother."

Abad's heart sinks a little, sensing the gravity in Azal's tone. They step into the room, and Azal closes the door behind them.

Abad asked. "What's up, Azal?"

Azal pauses, searching for the right words. He's not one to meddle in others' affairs, but this time, he feels it's necessary.

Azal replied. "I heard about your date with Sneha. She seems like a great girl… but bro, have you thought about where this might lead?"

Abad hesitates, then nods slowly. "I know, man. She's Hindu, I'm Muslim. Our parents would never accept it."

Azal sighs, running a hand through his hair. "That's precisely what I'm worried about. I've been there, Abad. I know what it's like to care deeply for someone, only to have everything crumble because of things we can't control. The pressure... It's suffocating. I don't want you to go through what I did."

Abad looks at Azal, surprised by the vulnerability in his brother's voice. "I didn't know it was that bad for you."

Azal nods, his eyes darkening with memories. "It was. I was in love, Abad, but in the end, it wasn't enough. Our families, society... they tore us apart. And I was left... broken. I don't want that for you. I don't want you to end up depressed like I did."

There's a heavy silence as Abad absorbs Azal's words. He respects Azal deeply, and seeing this side of him—one filled with pain and regret—makes Abad's own feelings all the more complicated.

Abad asked with disappointment on his face. "So, what should I do? Walk away now before it gets too serious?"

Azal shakes his head, surprising Abad. "No, brother. I'm not telling you to walk away. I'm telling you to be careful. But also... to be brave. You have something special with Sneha, and if you think it's worth fighting for, then do it. Don't make the same mistake I did by giving up too soon."

Abad looks at Azal, a mix of confusion and determination on his face. "You think I should go for it?"

Azal places a hand on Abad's shoulder, his expression softening. "Yes. Explore your love. I'm here to support you, no matter what happens. I lost in my battle, but I won't let you lose in yours."

Abad felt a wave of gratitude and a renewed sense of purpose. "Thanks, Azal. I won't let you down."

Later that evening, Abad shared this conversation with the group. Everyone listens intently, and when he recounts Azal's words, there's a collective sense of admiration for Azal. They all see a side of him they hadn't before—something deep and profoundly human.

I patted Azal's back and said. "Azal, man… we've always known you were strong, but this… this is something else."

Azal shrugs, trying to downplay it, but there's a glimmer of emotion in his eyes. "Just don't mess it up brother, alright?"

Chapter-12

As the days pass, my connection with Zoya continues to deepen. We started spending more time together, studying late into the night at the library and sharing meals in the canteen. There's a comfortable rhythm to our interactions, and though neither of us has said anything about love, it's clear that something special is brewing.

One evening, after a particularly intense study session, we both decided to take a break. Sitting under the stars in the MBA garden, we shared a quiet moment, sipping on milkshakes.

Zoya suddenly said. "You know, I never thought studying could be this... enjoyable."

I chuckled, feeling a warmth in your chest. "Guess it's the company."

Zoya smiles, a soft, almost shy expression that makes your heart skip a beat. There's silence , but it's not uncomfortable. It's the kind of silence that speaks volumes, where words aren't necessary to convey what's in my heart .

I said. "Zoya... you know I love you...right?"

Zoya looks at you, her eyes searching for yours. "Yeah, I know."

Zoya leaned her head on my shoulder, and we both sat there, quietly enjoying each other's company, the night wrapping around us like a blanket.

As the weeks passed, my bond with Zoya only grew stronger. What started as a comfortable friendship is now layered with something more—a connection that neither of us has fully acknowledged but both felt deeply. It's in the small things, like the way our hands brush when reaching for the same book or how our conversations flow so easily, even when we're just sitting in silence together.

One evening, after a long day of studying, Zoya and I decided to take a walk around campus. The night air is cool, and the campus is peaceful, with only the rustle of leaves accompanying our footsteps. As we walk, our conversation drifts from the usual academic talk to something more personal.

"Do you ever think about the future? Like, where will we be after all this?" I asked, trying to keep my voice casual.

Zoya looks over at me, her eyes thoughtful. "All the time. I wonder where life will take us, what paths we'll choose... if we'll still be in each other's lives."

There's a note of vulnerability in her voice that catches me off guard. I realize that, despite her calm exterior, Zoya has some serious problems in her life that I fear I don't know.

"I hope we are," I said, the words came out more honestly than I intended. "I mean, I can't imagine not having you around, Zoya. You've become... really important to me."

Zoya stops walking and turns to face me, her eyes searching mine. For a moment, it feels like the world around us fades away, leaving just the two of us standing there, caught in this moment.

"You're important to me too," she said softly, and I could hear the sincerity in her voice. "More than I've let on."

Her words hit me in a way I wasn't expecting. It's not that I didn't know she cared—I've felt it in the way she's always there, in the quiet moments we shared. But hearing it aloud makes it feel more real.

"I think about us a lot, Zoya," I admit, feeling a knot of nerves in my stomach. "About what we could be. But I don't want to rush you… or us."

Zoya gave me a small, almost shy smile that made my heart skip a beat. "I appreciate that. And I want to be honest with you too. I care about you… more than I expected to."

Without thinking, I reach out and take her hand, giving it a gentle squeeze. "I get that. And I'm not going anywhere. We'll figure this out together, at our own pace."

Zoya squeezes my hand back, and we continue our walk, now hand in hand. There's a quiet understanding between us, a mutual agreement that whatever this is, it's worth taking the time to nurture.

Chapter-13

The excitement for society interviews buzzed through our group like electricity. We each had our aspirations, and the societies we chose reflected those dreams. Riya, with her tall, model-like figure and effortless grace, naturally gravitated towards the fashion society. She had always carried herself with a confidence that turned heads wherever she went, and it was no surprise that she wanted to pursue modeling.

Preeti was interested in anchoring, so she decided to go for the calliope society. Abad, ever the cricket fanatic, didn't hesitate to sign up for the cricket society. It was his passion, his calling, and nothing made him happier than being on the field. Azal, usually the quietest among us, surprised everyone by filling out a form for "Khwashien," a poetry-based society. We'd only recently discovered that he wrote poems—deep, thoughtful verses that revealed a side of him we never knew existed.

Aryan, with his well-built physique and chiseled features, also opted for the fashion society. His ambitions leaned towards modeling, and with his looks, he had a real shot. Siddhart, the life of our group with his smooth dance moves, chose the dance society without a second thought. It was where he truly came alive.

Zoya, ever the intellectual, chose the debate society. She had a sharp mind and a way with words that left everyone in awe during discussions. And then there was me—I chose the organizing committee. It was the backbone of every event at KIIT, the society that made everything happen. Being a part of it meant responsibility, leadership, and a chance to make a real impact.

Our interviews were set for different times, but mine was at 7 AM—the earliest of them all. It was a Sunday, the one day we all craved to sleep in, but for me, that wasn't an option. The pressure of the interview weighed on me, yet excitement coursed through my veins.

Saturday night, instead of getting some much-needed rest, I found myself on a call with Zoya, Preeti, and Riya. We started talking about everything and nothing, eventually landing on the absurd idea of how the boys could sneak into the girls' hostel for a movie night by climbing the tree near Preeti and Zoya's window. It was a ridiculous plan, but we laughed about it, imagining the impossible.

Zoya, ever the sensible one, kept urging me to go to bed. "You need to wake up at 5 AM," she reminded me, her voice a blend of concern and teasing.

"Just five more minutes," I'd say, but those minutes stretched into hours. Before I knew it, the clock struck 3 AM, and Zoya's reminders turned into gentle pushes for me to get some sleep.

"Go on, sleep," she insisted, her voice softer now, almost like a lullaby. "You need to be at your best tomorrow."

Finally, I gave in, hanging up the call with a smile on my face. But in my exhaustion, I forgot the most crucial thing—setting my alarm.

The world was still dark when my phone rang, pulling me from the depths of sleep. I groggily reached for it, barely registering who could be calling at this hour. When I saw Zoya's name on the screen, a wave of confusion washed over me—until I remembered the interview.

"Wake up, sleepyhead." Her voice was the first thing I heard, soft yet firm, like she knew I would have slept through the entire morning if it weren't for her call.

"Zoya…?" I mumbled, still half-asleep, trying to grasp what was happening. And then it hit me—she had actually stayed up to make sure I didn't oversleep.

I couldn't help but smile, the warmth of her gesture seeping into my very bones. "You stayed up all night… for me?" I asked, a mix of surprise and admiration in my voice.

There was a brief pause before she replied, and I could hear the smile in her voice. "Well, someone had to make sure you didn't sleep through your big interview. Plus… I wanted to be the first to wish you good luck."

Her words touched something deep inside me, something that went beyond friendship. It wasn't just that she cared—it was the way she cared, with a thoughtfulness that felt almost intimate.

"Zoya… I don't know what to say," I began, feeling a lump form in my throat. "I really love that you did this for me. It means more than you know."

I could almost see her blushing on the other end of the line. "Don't make a big deal out of it," she said, trying to sound nonchalant but failing. "I just… didn't want you to mess this up."

Her voice softened, and I could tell she was trying to downplay it, but the emotion behind her words was unmistakable. She cared—deeply.

"Thank you," I said, my voice barely a whisper. "Really."

Zoya sighed, the kind of sigh that carries a mix of relief and exhaustion. "I'm just so tired now… I didn't sleep all night, just to make sure you'd wake up."

Guilt pricked at me. "You should go back to sleep," I urged. "Your interview isn't until 12 PM. You can sleep until 11 if you like."

"I'll try," she replied, her voice laced with sleepiness. "But I wanted to make sure you were okay first."

The tenderness in her words was almost overwhelming. This wasn't just about the interview—this was about us, about something growing between us that neither of us had fully acknowledged yet. It was in the little things she did, like staying up all night just to wake me up, that I saw how much she cared.

"You're amazing, you know that?" I said, trying to convey everything I was feeling in those few words.

There was a soft laugh on the other end. "Just go ace that interview, okay? I'm rooting for you."

"I will," I promised, feeling a surge of determination. "And then I'll call you as soon as it's done."

"Good," she replied, her voice already drifting into that dreamy tone that comes just before sleep takes over. "Good luck…"

As the call ended, I lay there for a moment, holding the phone to my chest, feeling a warmth that had nothing to do with the blankets. Zoya was looking out for me in a way that went beyond simple friendship, and it made me realize just how much I didn't want to lose this—whatever this was.

With a renewed sense of purpose, I got up, ready to face the day, knowing that regardless of what happened, I had someone who believed in me. And that made all the difference.

Chapter-14

The day had finally come, the one where everything we'd been talking about, dreaming about, and stressing over would either fall into place or shatter into a million pieces. We all knew Riya and Aryan were shoo-ins for the fashion society, but that didn't take away from the tension in the air. We gathered in the auditorium, our hearts racing as we watched each of our friends take the stage one by one, each of us silently rooting for the others while dealing with our own nerves.

Riya was up first. As she walked onto the stage, it was as if the entire room held its breath. She looked absolutely stunning, dressed in a way that highlighted every graceful curve, her long legs making her seem like she was gliding rather than walking. The flick of her hair, the subtle yet confident sway in her hips—every move she made sent a ripple of energy through the audience. You could practically feel the envy from the other girls and the admiration, mixed with longing, from the guys. They all wanted to be the one to hold her hand, to claim her as theirs. But Riya? She owned that stage like it was her kingdom, and she was the queen. The judges barely had to ask her any questions; her presence alone was enough to seal the deal.

Aryan followed, and though the pressure was on, he handled it like a pro. He didn't just walk the ramp—he made it his own. With a confident grin plastered on his face, he casually flexed his biceps as he strode forward, and the audience ate it up. His confidence was infectious, and before we knew it, the judges had made their decision. Aryan was in, just like we all knew he would be.

Then it was Azal's turn. He wasn't flashy like Riya or Aryan, but when he walked up with that little notebook in hand wearing a plain white kurta and blue jeans, you could see the intensity in his eyes. He recited his poem with a voice that carried the weight of all the emotions he'd poured into it:

"Mai chahoo bhi to tumko pa nahi sakta, aur ye baat kisi ko samjha nahi sakta."

The room went silent. Each word hung in the air, heavy with unspoken pain and longing. By the time he was done, there wasn't a dry eye in the room. The judges were moved—no, they were awestruck. Azal wasn't just accepted; he was celebrated, his raw talent undeniable.

Abad's cricket trials were next. On the field, he was a force to be reckoned with. Every swing of his bat, every precise shot, reminded me of why he was the best. The selectors didn't need any more proof; Abad was in, and the grin on his face as he walked off the field told me he knew it too.

Siddhart was a different story altogether. He took to the dance floor with a confidence that could only come from hours of practice. Dancing to the rhythm of "Bye Bye Bye" from the latest Deadpool movie, he nailed every move with such precision and flair that the dance society didn't hesitate for a second. Siddhart's spot was secured, and I couldn't help but feel a swell of pride for my friend.

Preeti was up for the anchoring trials, and she decided to go with stand-up comedy. Her humor was dark, unapologetically so, and as she delivered each punchline, the judges doubled over in laughter. Preeti had them in the palm of her hand, and by the end of her routine, they were practically begging her to join.

Zoya's turn came, and she chose a topic that resonated with everyone: equal rights for everyone. Her voice was steady, her arguments sharp, and the passion behind her words was undeniable. She didn't just speak; she commanded the room, and when she was done, there was no doubt in anyone's mind that she had nailed it.

And then, it was my turn.

I walked into the room, my heart pounding in my chest. I wore a plain white shirt, black formal pants, and my black Chelsea boots—an outfit that made me feel sharp, ready. The judges, a group of seasoned fourth-year students, watched me closely as I entered. I greeted them, trying to keep my voice steady, and they asked me to introduce myself. I did, keeping it brief but confident.

Then came the questions. Why was I opting for the organizing committee? Did I have any experience in this field? I could feel their eyes on me, waiting for any sign of hesitation. But I didn't give them any. "It's my first time," I admitted, "but I know for sure that if you want the work done in time, I'm the man you want by your side." I could see a flicker of interest in their eyes, and that gave me the boost I needed.

Next, they asked me to rate myself out of 10 in leadership. Without missing a beat, I said, "I'm a 9."

"Why not 10?" one of them asked, leaning forward slightly.

I smiled, trying to keep the nerves from showing. "There's always room for improvement. No man is perfect, and I'm joining this society to improve myself and give something back."

They exchanged glances, impressed. I walked out of that room feeling like I had done all I could, but the nerves didn't leave. The next week was a blur of classes and late-night talks with Zoya, trying to distract myself from the waiting. But finally, the results came out. One by one, we checked our names, and the relief that washed over me when I saw mine was indescribable. We had all made it.

That day in class, we couldn't contain our excitement. The boys and I came up with a plan, one that had been brewing since our late-night chat—breaking into the girls' hostel for a party bash in Preeti and Zoya's room. It was risky, but the thrill of it was too tempting to resist. We knew it was reckless, but after everything we'd just accomplished, we felt invincible.

Chapter-15

The night was electric as we gathered beneath the girls' hostel, our excitement palpable. Aryan's confident climb set the stage, and Siddhart followed with a focused determination that heightened the anticipation. Each branch creaked beneath our weight, adding to the thrill of our rule-breaking adventure.

When I reached the window, Zoya's face appeared, her eyes wide with a mix of excitement and concern. Her touch was a reassuring jolt, and as I climbed through, the adrenaline transformed into a different kind of thrill. Inside, Preeti was busy setting up with a mischievous grin, the warm, golden light of the room making everything feel inviting. Sneha's unexpected arrival caused a stir. Abad's eyes widened in shock as he saw her, a mix of surprise and delight on his face. Riya, with a playful wink, had called Sneha to join us, adding an unexpected spark to the evening.

"Wow, Sneha, and I didn't expect to see you here!" Abad exclaimed, his voice tinged with genuine astonishment and happiness.

Sneha laughed, her eyes twinkling. "Riya pulled me in with her charm. I couldn't resist the chance to join the fun."

The room buzzed with renewed energy. Abad, still recovering from his surprise, tried to act nonchalant, but his excitement was evident. Riya moved through the group, her lively demeanor bringing us all closer together.

Azal, who had been quietly observing, stepped into the conversation with his usual calm demeanor. "Looks like things just got a lot more interesting," he said with a smile, his eyes glinting with curiosity.

Siddhart, always the energetic one, nudged Azal playfully. "You're just saying that because you're hoping for some extra drama tonight."

Azal chuckled, shaking his head. "I just appreciate the unpredictability. Keeps things exciting."

As the evening progressed, the tension in the room grew. The thrill of rebellion and the thrill of new connections created a charged atmosphere. Zoya and Preeti took their first puffs of cigarettes, their reactions eliciting peals of laughter from the group. Zoya's initial coughing fit only added to the shared amusement.

I nudged Aryan, a grin on my face. "Come on, man, take off your shirt and show us what you've got. It's a party, after all."

Aryan hesitated but soon relented. As he removed his shirt, revealing his well-defined chest, the room's energy shifted. Preeti's gaze lingered on him, her admiration turning into something deeper. She reached out and touched his chest, the brief contact sending a thrill through both of them. Her blush deepened, and her breath hitched slightly, the moment was charged with unspoken attraction.

Sneha's laughter and charm blended seamlessly with the group, her presence adding a light-hearted touch to the evening. As the party continued, the interactions became more intense. Riya and Preeti exchanged knowing glances, their excitement palpable. Zoya, ever the practical one, kept an eye on the time, her concern for our potential discovery evident.

As the evening progressed, the atmosphere grew more charged. Someone suggested a game that would add a new twist to the night's adventure. The rules were simple: each couple would take turns kissing, a playful challenge that promised both fun and deeper connections.

Aryan and Preeti were up first. The tension between them was palpable, and their hesitation was clear. They stood side by side, their nervous glances betraying their uncertainty about their feelings. The group's encouragement grew louder, mixing with playful cheers.

"You guys should totally go for it," I urged, sensing the moment's potential. "You never know what might happen if you don't take the chance."

After a few moments of coaxing, Aryan and Preeti finally leaned in. Their kiss was tentative at first but quickly grew more confident. As their lips met, a spark ignited, and they pulled away with a shared realization of the connection they had felt from the beginning. The kiss was more than just a playful gesture; it was a confirmation of something deeper that had been building between them.

Sneha and Abad were next. Sneha's eyes met Abad's with a mix of mischief and affection. Abad's initial nervousness melted away as Sneha's charm and warmth enveloped him. Their kiss was tender, a reflection of the unexpected but genuine feelings that had surfaced over the course of the evening. Azal, observing from a distance, kept his gaze averted, his demeanor unchanged despite the unfolding intimacy.

Riya and Siddhart followed, their kiss full of spontaneity and passion. The intensity between them was evident, their shared moment a burst of energy that electrified the room. The group's cheers grew louder, their excitement palpable.

The final round of the game brought the focus back to me and Zoya. The room's atmosphere shifted as everyone turned their attention to us, their voices a blend of anticipation and encouragement.

"Come on, kiss her!" someone called out, the excitement in their tone undeniable.

Zoya's eyes widened, a mix of fear and thrill crossing her face. She looked at me, her emotions clearly on display. I could see her heart racing, her expression a whirlwind of apprehension and hope.

"Hey, it's okay," I said softly, my voice steady despite the mounting tension. "We don't have to do anything you're not comfortable with."

Zoya's relief was palpable. Her shoulders relaxed, and a grateful smile touched her lips. She looked at me with a newfound understanding, her eyes reflecting the depth of her emotions. In that moment, she realized that my feelings for her were genuine—that I liked her for who she truly was, not just as part of the game.

Although we didn't kiss, the air was charged with an intense, unspoken connection. Our emotions swirled around us, creating a moment that was as powerful as any kiss could have been. The night's events had revealed the layers of our feelings and deepened our bond, leaving us both with a profound sense of closeness and understanding.

As the game wound down and the group's laughter and chatter faded, the intimacy of the moment lingered. We had navigated a night of daring adventures and emotional revelations, and as we settled back into the relaxed atmosphere of the room, it was clear that our connections had grown stronger, more authentic, and more meaningful.

Chapter-16

The aftermath of the party left everyone buzzing with excitement. Laughter and chatter filled the room as the group talked about the night's events. Aryan and Preeti, still reeling from their kiss, found themselves drawn to each other more than ever. However, the mood shifted when Preeti's phone buzzed with an incoming call.

Preeti glanced at the screen and frowned. "It's him again," she muttered under her breath, but Aryan noticed the worried look on her face.

"Who's calling?" Aryan asked, his curiosity piqued.

"Just… someone I'd rather not talk about," Preeti replied, trying to brush it off.

Over the coming days, the calls from Preeti's ex-boyfriend, Aditya, intensified. He was from Mumbai, the city where Preeti had lived before coming to college. The messages were filled with threats and accusations. Aryan grew increasingly concerned as he noticed Preeti's growing distress and her reluctance to share details.

One evening, as they sat together studying, Aryan finally confronted her. "Preeti, what's going on? You've been so distant lately. Is this about your ex?"

Preeti hesitated, her eyes welling up with tears. "He's been calling me. Harassing me. He found out about us, and… he's trying to scare me, manipulate me. I didn't want to tell you because I didn't want you to get involved."

Aryan's face darkened with anger and hurt. "Why didn't you tell me sooner? Do you still have feelings for him?"

"No, Aryan!" Preeti protested, her voice trembling. "I just... I didn't want to drag you into this mess."

As the harassment continued, Aryan's frustration grew. He felt betrayed and confused, struggling to understand Preeti's feelings and Aditya's motives. The stress from the situation began to affect their interactions. Aryan became withdrawn, and Preeti's anxiety made her snappy and distant. Their arguments grew frequent and heated. She felt trapped between her fear and her love for Aryan.

Determined to put an end to the harassment, Aryan suggested taking a more direct approach. "I want to talk to him. Maybe if he sees I'm serious about being with you, he'll back off."

Preeti immediately shook her head. "No, Aryan. It's not safe. He's volatile and manipulative. Talking to him might make things worse. We need to handle this carefully."

Despite his frustration, Aryan reluctantly agreed to let Preeti handle it her way. She decided to confront Aditya herself and called him. The conversation quickly turned ugly, with Aditya spewing anger and abusive language. Preeti tried to stay calm, but Aryan, listening nearby, couldn't bear it anymore.

Grabbing the phone from Preeti, Aryan spoke firmly into the receiver. "Listen, Aditya, this ends now. If you so much as think about bothering Preeti again, you'll have to deal with me. Understand?"

There was silence on the other end, and then Aditya muttered something before hanging up.

Preeti looked at Aryan, tears filling her eyes. "I should have trusted you from the beginning. I'm so sorry."

Aryan's expression softened, and he cupped her face in his hands. "I would destroy anyone who threatens you. You're safe with me, Preeti."

Overwhelmed with emotion, Preeti couldn't hold back her tears. She threw her arms around Aryan, and in that moment, all the fear and tension melted away. They kissed, sealing their bond with a new depth of trust and love.

The rest of the group eventually learned about the situation, and their reactions varied. Some were supportive, others were critical, but the overall consensus was that Aryan and Preeti had shown remarkable resilience. The group rallied around them, offering support and advice.

As the chapter closed, Aryan and Preeti's relationship emerged stronger from the ordeal. The challenges they faced had deepened their bond, and they were more committed to each other than ever.

Chapter-17

The hostel was quiet, with most students either asleep or engrossed in their own late-night activities. I wandered through the dimly lit paths, the cool breeze brushing against my skin. As I rounded a corner, I spotted Azal standing alone near the edge of the hostel courtyard, the faint glow of a cigarette illuminating his face.

Deciding to join him, I walked over, the smell of smoke greeting me as I approached. He looked up, acknowledging my presence with a nod but didn't say anything. I stood beside him in silence for a moment, watching the cigarette burn down slowly.

"Does it help ease the pain?" I finally asked, breaking the silence.

Azal took a long drag, exhaled slowly, and shook his head. "No. Not really."

"Then why do you smoke?" I pressed.

Azal flicked the ash off the end of his cigarette, staring at it as if it held all the answers. "Because... when I was at my lowest, this was the only thing by my side. The only thing that didn't judge, didn't leave."

I sighed, feeling a pang of sadness for him. "Dipshit, we're here for you. Everyone. You're not alone."

He looked at me, a hint of a smile tugging at the corners of his lips, but his eyes remained distant. "I know, brother. I do. But still... It eases the pain somehow. Not properly, not fully, but a little."

I watched him take another drag, the smoke curling up into the night sky. We had shared a few cigarettes over the past few weeks, usually during late-night conversations like this. But something about tonight felt different. The weight of his words, the weariness in his voice—it was heavier than usual.

"You know," I started, choosing my words carefully, "we've had a few smokes together over the past few weeks, but maybe it's time to stop."

Azal chuckled softly, but it was a hollow sound, devoid of humor. "I can't."

"Why not?" I asked, genuinely concerned.

He paused, the cigarette halfway to his lips, as if searching for the right words. His expression grew darker, more introspective. "One day you'll understand, brother. One day."

We stood in silence, the only sound the occasional crackle of the cigarette as Azal took another drag. The night felt colder now, and I found myself wishing I could find the right words to break through the wall he had built around himself.

Finally, I spoke again, my voice quieter, more tentative. "You know I'm here for you, right? Whenever you're ready... to talk, to let it out... I'm here."

Azal nodded, but his eyes were distant, lost in a place I couldn't reach. "I know. And I appreciate it. But some things... some things can't be fixed with words. Some things... i just need time."

His words lingered in the air, leaving a sense of unease between us. The conversation had taken a darker turn than I had anticipated, and I could feel the tension in Azal, a storm brewing just beneath the surface.

As the cigarette burned down to its filter, Azal flicked it away, watching as the ember faded into the darkness. He turned to me, his expression softening slightly. "Thanks for staying with me tonight."

"Anytime," I replied, trying to muster a smile. But the unease still gnawed at me. "Just… don't shut us out, okay? We're your friends. We care about you."

Azal's eyes met mine, and for a brief moment, I saw a flicker of something—gratitude, maybe, or perhaps regret. "I won't. Promise."

But as he turned and walked away, I couldn't shake the feeling that there was something more, something he wasn't telling me. And as much as I wanted to help, I knew that whatever it was, it would be up to him to face it, in his own time.

Chapter-18

Azal and Abad were born in Hazaribagh, a small town in Jharkhand, into a conservative Muslim family. Growing up as twin brothers, they were inseparable, sharing everything from childhood secrets to teenage ambitions. Their father was a respected figure in the local community, and their mother was deeply involved in raising the twins with strong cultural and religious values. The family was close-knit, and the brothers were taught to uphold their traditions and respect their heritage.

From an early age, both Azal and Abad showed promise in their studies, earning them admiration from their teachers and peers. Azal, the quieter and more introspective of the two, was drawn to literature and poetry, finding solace in words and expressions. Abad, on the other hand, was passionate about sports, particularly cricket, where he excelled as a player. Despite their different interests, the twins were each other's strongest supporters, and they dreamed of making their mark in the world—Azal as a writer and Abad as a cricketer.

During their school years, Azal fell in love with Manisha, a Hindu girl from his class. Their relationship blossomed quickly, with Manisha becoming a source of happiness for Azal amidst the pressures of school life. However, their love was met with fierce opposition from both their families, who could not accept the idea of a Muslim-Hindu relationship. The cultural and religious differences were deemed insurmountable, and despite the love they shared, Manisha's family pressured her to end the relationship. Azal's own family, fearing the societal backlash, also urged him to break it off.

Abad, who had always been Azal's confidant, tried to support his brother during this painful time. He understood the depth of Azal's love for Manisha and the agony of being torn apart due to their families' rigid beliefs. Abad's own experience with societal expectations, particularly the pressure to succeed in cricket to bring honor to his family, gave him a unique perspective on the situation. However, even Abad's support couldn't prevent the inevitable—Manisha, under immense pressure from her family, ended the relationship, leaving Azal heartbroken.

The breakup was devastating for Azal. He withdrew from those around him, including Abad, and became more reserved, burying his emotions behind a wall of stoicism. This period of his life marked the beginning of his smoking habit, a way to numb the pain and fill the void left by Manisha. The cigarette became his silent companion, the only thing that didn't judge or abandon him during his lowest moments.

Abad, though deeply concerned for his brother, had his own battles to fight. As he pursued his cricket dreams, he found himself caught between his passion and the expectations placed upon him. While he wanted to be there for Azal, the demands of his sport often pulled him away, leading to feelings of guilt and helplessness.

Chapter-19

The day felt unusually heavy without Zoya's presence in class. Every glance toward her empty seat filled me with unease. After the lecture, I couldn't resist anymore; I had to know where she was. Approaching Preeti, I tried to mask my concern, but it slipped through. "Where's Zoya? She's never missed a class."

Preeti sighed, her voice laced with worry. "She's down with a fever and a bad cold. She's resting in the hostel."

Hearing that sent a pang through me. Zoya, my strong, independent Zoya, confined to bed, unwell? The thought lingered in my mind all day. As soon as classes ended, I met Preeti outside the hostel. I had already called for a cab, determined to make sure Zoya got the care she needed. Together, we took her to a local doctor. The visit was quick, the diagnosis simple: rest and medication. But seeing her pale and tired in the doctor's office, I knew this was more than just about medicine. She needed to feel cared for, loved even.

Back at the college, Preeti helped Zoya settle back into bed. I watched from the doorway, feeling helpless yet determined. I wanted to do more, to be there for her in a way that made a difference. Reluctantly, I headed back to my room, my thoughts completely consumed by her.

An hour passed, and I couldn't focus on anything. Zoya was all I could think about. I picked up my phone and called her, needing to hear her voice, to know she was okay. "Hey, how are you feeling? Do you want to eat something?"

Her voice came through the receiver, soft and weak. "I'm okay, just tired. But... I kind of want to eat mangoes."

"Mangoes?" I asked, surprised. "It's almost October, Zoya. They're out of season."

"I know," she said with a little laugh. "It's impossible, right?"

Her tone was playful, almost teasing, but I heard the longing in it. Something inside me clicked, and I knew I couldn't let her down. Without telling her, I put on my shoes and headed out, determined to find mangoes in a city where they should have been long gone.

For two hours, I combed through every market, and every fruit vendor in Bhubaneswar, searching. Just when I was about to give up, I found a small cold storage facility that had a batch of unsold mangoes. They were fresh, probably left over from the last harvest. My heart soared as I bought them, not caring how much they cost. I just wanted to see the smile on her face when she got them.

By 8 PM, I was back at the college, exhausted but satisfied. I called Preeti to check on Zoya, only to find out she still hadn't eaten anything. "She doesn't want dinner," Preeti said, clearly concerned.

"Perfect," I said, hanging up, a plan forming in my mind.

Sneaking around the hostel was something I had become somewhat accustomed to, and tonight was no different. I climbed the tree beside Zoya's window and knocked gently, hoping she'd be awake. The window opened slowly, and there she was—Zoya, with her hair slightly tousled, and her eyes tired but alert.

She blinked in surprise when she saw me standing there with a polythene bag in hand. "Fawaz? What are you doing here? What's in the bag?"

I smiled, holding it out to her. "Is that what I think it is?" she asked, her eyes widening with disbelief.

"Yes, dear," I replied, unable to hide my excitement.

Her face lit up in a way that made my heart skip a beat. She reached out, took the bag from me, and peeked inside. When she saw the mangoes, her tiredness seemed to vanish. She clapped her hands together like a little child, her joy so pure and contagious. "You really found them!" she exclaimed, her voice filled with happiness.

Watching her like that, so full of life despite her illness, something stirred deep within me. As she savored each bite, her eyes closing in delight, I knew it with certainty—she was the one I wanted to be with, the one I wanted to protect, to make happy, no matter what it took.

"No one's ever done this for me before," she said softly, looking up at me with those deep, soulful eyes. There was something vulnerable about her in that moment, something that made my heart swell with a protective instinct.

"I'd do anything for you, Zoya," I found myself saying, the words slipping out before I could think.

She smiled, a small, genuine smile that made me feel like the world was right, even if just for a moment. After she finished eating, I helped her to the washbasin to clean up, and just as we were finishing, Preeti, Riya, and Sneha walked in. Their eyes widened in surprise at seeing me there, but the shock quickly turned to something else as Zoya told them about what I had done.

"I wish Siddhart was like you," Riya teased, making us all laugh. The tension in the room melted away, replaced by a warmth that only comes from shared moments like these.

After a while, I knew it was time for me to leave. I slipped out the window, leaving the girls to their chatter. But as they started talking, I couldn't help but overhear their conversation through the open window.

Riya, Sneha, and Preeti praised me to Zoya, and it filled me with a quiet sense of pride. "He's really a great guy, Zoya. He's got all the green flags," Riya said. "It's been almost three months, and he's shown no red flags."

Preeti, who was clearly happy with Aryan, added, "If I were in your place, I'd never have the opportunity to make Fawaz my boyfriend."

Zoya was silent, taking it all in. I could imagine her sitting there, considering their words, knowing deep down that they were right. But still, something was holding her back, something she wasn't ready to share.

That night, she called me again, her voice soft, filled with a mix of gratitude and something else I couldn't quite place. "Thank you, Fawaz," she whispered. "For everything."

"You don't have to thank me, Zoya," I replied, my heart aching with the desire to say more, to tell her how much she meant to me.

We talked for a long time, the conversation weaving between light banter and deeper, more emotional topics. There was a tenderness in her voice, a vulnerability that she rarely showed. I could tell she wanted to be with me, to let herself fall, but something was stopping her.

"Zoya," I said gently, "what's holding you back? Why can't you let me in?"

There was a long pause, and I could hear her struggling with her emotions. "I can't, Fawaz… not right now. Please don't ask me why."

Her words cut deep, but I respected her too much to push. Instead, I tried to comfort her in the only way I knew how.

"Just say the word, and we'll take on the world. Just say you're hurt, we'll face the worst,"

I sang softly, the lyrics a promise of my unwavering support. On the other end, I heard her start to cry, the sound breaking my heart. "Please don't ever leave me alone," she said, her voice trembling with emotion.

"I won't," I replied, my voice thick with emotion. "You know I love you, right?"

"I know," she said, her voice barely above a whisper. The words, though they held no promise of more, were still filled with meaning. She knew, and that was enough for now.

It was hard not to feel a twinge of disappointment, but I had promised her I wouldn't push, and I intended to keep that promise. "Take care of yourself," I said softly. "And skip tomorrow's class too. You need the rest."

"No," she insisted, a hint of her usual stubbornness returning. "I want to attend. The midterms are near."

I couldn't help but smile at that, admiring her determination. "Alright," I said, "but if you feel unwell, promise me you'll rest."

“I promise,” she said, and with that, we said our goodnights, the conversation leaving me with a heart full of love, but also a deep, unspoken longing.

As I lay in bed that night, I couldn’t shake the feeling that something was going to change between us. What was holding her back? And when would she finally let me in? These questions swirled in my mind, keeping me awake long after we had hung up, the uncertainty both thrilling and terrifying. But one thing was clear—I was falling deeper for Zoya with every passing day, and I wasn’t going to give up on her, no matter what.

Chapter-20

The pond on campus was a serene refuge, its still waters mirroring the deepening hues of twilight. The sky was a canvas of velvety indigo, speckled with stars that began to pierce the darkness. It was around 7 PM, and Zoya and I had settled into our usual spot beside the pond, finding comfort in our shared presence.

Tonight, however, an unusual quiet had settled over us. The usual easy banter was replaced by a heavy silence. We had drifted into our own thoughts, the world outside seeming to fade away. The gentle rustling of leaves and the soft ripple of water provided a soothing backdrop.

Without breaking the silence, Zoya leaned her head against my shoulder. The gesture was tender, an unspoken request for closeness. I wrapped my arm around her, pulling her in gently. Her warmth and the softness of her presence felt like a balm to my soul.

Moments later, I felt a slight tremor in her body. The smooth rhythm of her breaths became irregular, and I realized she was crying. My heart tightened at the sight of her distress. I turned to her, my voice full of concern. "Zoya, what's wrong?"

She didn't answer immediately. Her sobs were muffled against my shoulder, each breath coming out in uneven gasps. I could feel her tears soaking into my shirt, and it tore at my heart. "Please, tell me what's happening. I'm here for you."

Her crying seemed to intensify, and I felt helpless. I gently stroked her hair, trying to offer some semblance of comfort. "You don't have to go through this alone. Whatever it is, we can face it together."

After what felt like an eternity, she managed to speak, her voice quivering. "Fawaz, I didn't want to burden you with this. I've been holding so much inside, and it's so hard to talk about..."

I shifted to face her fully, my hands cupping her face gently. "You don't have to hide anything from me. I want to understand. I want to be here for you, no matter what."

Zoya looked up at me, her eyes reflecting the starlight and the depth of her fear. "I'm scared, Fawaz. Scared of getting close to anyone and every time I let someone in, they end up getting hurt. It's like a cycle I can't break. I'm terrified of losing you too."

The pain in her voice was palpable, and it broke my heart to hear her vulnerability. I pulled her into a tight embrace, holding her close. "Zoya, you're not going to lose me. I'm here, and I'm not going anywhere. I care about you more than you know. You don't have to face this alone."

She clung to me, her tears mingling with her whispered confessions. "It's just so hard for me to trust. I want to, but I'm afraid. I don't want to push you away, but I'm also scared of getting hurt."

I kissed her forehead softly, feeling a deep sense of connection. As we sat there, the stars above seemed to shine brighter, casting a gentle light over us. The pond's ripples created a calming rhythm, and the night felt more intimate than ever. I held her close, feeling the steady beat of her heart against mine.

The world outside faded away, leaving only the two of us in our own cocoon of understanding and support. Zoya's breathing began to even out, and the tears gradually ceased. She leaned back into me, a sense of calm settling between us.

I kissed her temple gently, my heart swelling with love and commitment. The night grew deeper, and the stars continued their silent vigil. She started telling her back story.

Chapter-21

We sat by the pond, the stars reflecting off the still water as Zoya began to speak, her voice carrying the weight of years of pain and fear.

"My father was a big businessman in Lucknow," she began, her tone distant as if she were speaking from a memory far away. "He was everything to me, especially after my mother died when I was just ten. Losing her was hard, but I still had him. We were close—he used to call me his little princess. He was all I had, and I was all he had."

She paused, taking a deep breath as she continued, "But then, he remarried. I was too young to understand at first, but I knew from the start that something was wrong with her. Farida—that was her name—came into our lives like a storm. She was beautiful, yes, but cold. I could tell she didn't care about me, or even about him. All she wanted was what he had—his money, his status. And she brought her brother, Rauf, with her. He was... well, he was trouble from the start."

I noticed her hands trembling slightly as she spoke, so I gently reached out and held them, giving her the strength to continue.

"Farida never tried to be a mother to me. In fact, she did everything she could to push me aside, to make me feel unwanted in my own home. My father, blinded by grief or maybe just trying to move on, didn't see it—or maybe he didn't want to see it. He became distant, caught up in his business and in Farida's web of lies. And I was left alone, trying to survive in that house that no longer felt like a home."

She looked down, her voice wavering, "Then, when I was fifteen, everything changed. My father... he was murdered. The police said it was a robbery gone wrong, but I knew it was more than that. Farida didn't even pretend to be sad. She just took control—of the mansion, of the business, of everything. And I was trapped with her and Rauf, with no one to protect me."

Her grip on my hands tightened as she spoke about what happened next, her voice thick with emotion. "The mansion became a prison. Farida and Rauf—they did whatever they wanted. Rauf was a parasite, wasting my father's money on gambling, drinking, and all kinds of things. And Farida let him. She supported him, encouraged him even. And me? I was just in the way. They saw me as nothing but a nuisance, a reminder of the life they had stolen."

Tears welled up in her eyes, and I could see the pain she was reliving as she continued, "One day, Rauf... he... he sexually harassed me. It was the worst day of my life. I was so scared, so broken. I went to Farida, hoping she would help me, but she didn't. She didn't believe me. She accused me of lying, of trying to cause trouble. And then... she punished me for it. She protected him, her brother, and left me alone to deal with everything. I had no one, Fawaz. No one."

Her tears fell freely now, and I gently wiped them away, feeling my heart break for the girl she had been, trapped in that nightmare.

"I was a prisoner in that house," she whispered, her voice barely audible. "I wasn't allowed to leave, wasn't allowed to have friends or do anything normal. The only thing that kept me going was the money my father had saved for my education. He put it in a separate account, so Farida couldn't touch it. She didn't want me to leave for college at first—she wanted to keep me under her control. But eventually, she realized that with me gone, she could have full control over the mansion, over everything. So she let me go, thinking she was getting rid of a burden."

She looked at me then, her eyes filled with a mix of fear and hope. "But the scars, Fawaz... they never really healed. I've struggled to trust anyone since then. I'm always afraid that if I let someone in, they'll hurt me, just like Farida and Rauf did. It's like I'm still trapped in that house, even though I'm far away from it."

I pulled her into my arms, holding her close as she cried softly against my chest. "You're not alone anymore, Zoya," I whispered into her hair. "You don't have to carry this by yourself. I'm with you to the end of the line."

She clung to me, her body trembling as years of pain and fear spilled out in her tears. And as I held her, I silently vowed that I would do everything in my power to protect her, to show her that she was loved, and that she was safe with me.

The stars above us seemed to shine a little brighter, and for the first time, I felt like we were truly connected—not just by our shared moments, but by the understanding and trust that was beginning to form between us. Zoya had opened up a part of herself that she had kept hidden for so long, and I knew that from this moment on, things would never be the same.

Chapter-22

We remained by the pond, the tranquil water reflecting the starlit sky, but the peace of the scene felt like a distant memory. Zoya was trembling beside me, her earlier composure shattered by the unsettling encounter with Rauf. I could feel the weight of her fear and sadness pressing down on both of us.

"Zoya, we need to do something about this," I said, trying to keep my voice steady despite the growing turmoil inside me. "We should go to the police. They need to know what he's doing."

She shook her head, her eyes filled with a mix of fear and resignation. "No, Fawaz," she said, her voice trembling. "I can't go to the police. Justice isn't always served here. I don't want to be caught in a never-ending court case, and I don't have the courage or energy for that."

Her words hit me hard. I could see the pain in her eyes, the exhaustion from fighting a battle she felt she couldn't win. "But you can't just ignore this. You need protection," I insisted, trying to reach her through the cloud of fear and uncertainty.

Zoya's gaze dropped to the ground, her voice barely a whisper. "I don't want you to risk your career or get dragged into this mess. I appreciate your concern, but I don't want you to get hurt or caught up in something that could end badly."

I took her hands in mine, holding them gently but firmly. "Zoya, whatever you decide, I need you to know that if I see anything bad happening, I will react. I will protect you, no matter what. I may not have all the answers, but I can't just stand by and do nothing."

She looked up at me, tears welling in her eyes. "I know you will, Fawaz. That's what scares me. I'm afraid you'll get hurt because of me. I don't want to be the cause of more pain in your life."

I shook my head, my resolve unshaken. "We all are with you, Zoya. You don't have to go through this alone. We'll figure it out together."

Her eyes softened, and she took a deep breath, trying to calm herself. "I don't want anyone else to know about my past. I just want to be a normal girl here, without everyone knowing the baggage I carry."

I nodded, my voice filled with determination. "I promise, Zoya. No one will know about me. Your past is yours alone to share when you're ready."

With a deep breath, she took my hand and leaned closer, her head resting on my shoulder. The tears continued to fall, but there was a sense of relief in her posture. "Fawaz, I feel the same for you. I just didn't want you to carry my baggage. I was scared of how it would affect us."

The intensity of her emotions struck me deeply. I wrapped my arms around her, pulling her close. "Zoya, I'd die fighting for you," I said, my voice thick with emotion. "I would face any challenge, go through any storm, just to see you safe and happy."

In that moment, everything else faded away. The stars above, the gentle ripple of the pond, and the quiet night seemed to hold their breath as Zoya leaned in. Our lips met in a kiss that was both tender and full of unspoken promises. It was a kiss that conveyed everything we had shared—the pain, the love, and the hope for a future together.

When we finally pulled apart, I gently kissed her forehead, a gesture of deep affection and reassurance. "I'm here for you," I whispered. "Always and forever."

Zoya's eyes met mine, her expression a mixture of gratitude and something deeper, something that felt like a promise. "I love you, Fawaz," she said softly, her voice trembling with raw emotion.

"I love you too, Zoya," I replied, my heart swelling with an overwhelming sense of commitment and love. "We'll face everything together."

We stayed by the pond, holding each other close, finding solace in the quiet intimacy of the night. The world around us seemed to dissolve into the background as we embraced, knowing that no matter what challenges lay ahead, we would face them side by side, with an unbreakable bond of trust and love.

Chapter-23

The next morning, I was jolted awake by the sound of my phone ringing. Zoya's voice cut through the haze of sleep, commanding and sweet. "Fawaz, wake up! You've got class soon. We need to get moving."

Despite being an early riser only when absolutely necessary, I couldn't help but smile at her authoritative tone. It was one of those little things that made me appreciate her even more—her ability to be both commanding and caring. I grumbled in response, "Alright, I'm up."

Before I even had a chance to react, I pressed a quick, affectionate kiss to the phone, feeling a rush of warmth from the gesture. I clambered out of bed, reluctantly leaving the cozy confines of my blankets. As I took a shower, the upbeat tune of Darshan Rawal's "Pehla Pehla Pyaar" filled the room. I was in high spirits, energized by Zoya's wake-up call and the prospect of the day ahead.

Aryan burst into the bathroom, his usual relaxed demeanor replaced by curiosity. "You're up early for class," he said, eyeing me with an amused expression. "And what's with the song?"

I couldn't contain my grin. "You'll find out soon enough. Just feeling good this morning."

With Aryan's teasing comments behind us, we headed to the girls' hostel. The morning air was crisp, and the campus was slowly coming to life with the hustle and bustle of students. The anticipation of the day ahead added a touch of excitement to the atmosphere.

When we reached the girls' hostel, my gaze immediately found Zoya amidst the group of girls. She looked stunning. Her hair had a radiant shine that outshone the morning sun, and her face was glowing with a beauty that took my breath away. I felt a surge of pride and affection.

As Zoya noticed us, she walked over with a grace that seemed almost ethereal. She wrapped her arms around me in a warm hug, and then, without hesitation, she took my hand. It was a gesture filled with both affection and possessiveness, and I loved it. It was as if she was claiming a piece of her world with me in it.

"Come on," she said softly, pulling me towards the class.

Our friends watched us with a mixture of surprise and admiration. Preeti's eyes twinkled as she nudged Riya and whispered something that made them both smile. Abad, with his characteristic enthusiasm, gave me a thumbs-up. There was a palpable sense of camaraderie and celebration as we walked together.

Entering the classroom hand-in-hand with Zoya was a new and exhilarating experience. As we walked in, the room seemed to buzz with an electric energy. Zoya's presence was like a spotlight, drawing all eyes to us. I could feel the envious glances from the other boys, especially those who had admired Zoya from afar.

We chose a seat together, and I could sense the shift in the classroom dynamics. The usual chatter and laughter were replaced by murmurs and curious glances. Zoya's beauty and our open display of affection made us the center of attention.

It felt like a small victory to be with her, but I also sensed the weight of everyone's gaze. Zoya's hand was warm in mine, and it was comforting to feel her support. We sat together, our presence creating a subtle ripple of excitement and jealousy.

Among those watching was Ayush. Known for his flirtatious reputation and his habit of hitting on every girl he saw, Ayush had always had a particular interest in Zoya. His reaction to seeing her with me was both intense and telling.

His face, usually adorned with a confident smirk, now displayed a mix of surprise and dismay. The realization that Zoya was no longer available for his advances seemed to hit him hard. He tried to maintain his usual demeanor, but it was clear he was unsettled.

As he approached us after class began, his tone was forcedly casual, masking his underlying frustration. "Hey, Fawaz," he said, his eyes flicking between Zoya and me. "Zoya."

Zoya responded with a polite nod, while I met his gaze with a steady look. "Ayush."

He tried to engage in conversation, but his attempts were lackluster, revealing his irritation beneath the surface. His usual charm seemed absent, replaced by an awkwardness that made me feel a sense of satisfaction. I could tell that Ayush's ego had taken a hit, and it was hard not to enjoy the moment.

As the class went on, I could feel the tension in the air. The other boys' reactions ranged from jealous glares to whispered comments. It was clear that our relationship had stirred up a whirlwind of emotions among our peers.

Zoya seemed aware of the attention, and while she maintained her composure, I noticed a hint of discomfort. "Are you okay?" I asked softly, leaning in closer to her.

She gave me a reassuring smile, though it didn't fully reach her eyes. "I'm fine. Just feeling a bit uncomfortable with all the attention."

I squeezed her hand gently. "We'll face it together. Don't let it get to you."

As we left the classroom, Zoya and I walked side by side, navigating the day with a renewed sense of unity. Despite the challenges and the jealous stares, we found strength in each other's presence. The day had brought its share of tensions, but it had also solidified our bond and our commitment to facing whatever came our way together.

The mix of emotions—the pride, the jealousy, the admiration—created a complex tapestry of feelings that marked the beginning of a new chapter in our lives. As we walked through the campus, hand in hand, it was clear that we were ready to face the world together, no matter what challenges lay ahead.

Chapter-24

When I had to leave for home due to a family emergency, I was reluctant, but it was unavoidable. As much as I hated being away from Zoya, I trusted that everything would be fine for a few days. I didn't realize how much could change in such a short time.

Back home, I was caught up in the family situation, but Zoya was never far from my mind. During a quiet moment, I found myself showing her photo to my cousin, Fiza. Even though she was three years older than me, Fiza had always been like a sister—someone I could talk to about anything, including my love life. When she saw Zoya's photo, her eyes widened, and she let out a low whistle. "Wow, Fawaz. She's stunning. You've got yourself a keeper."

I couldn't help but smile proudly. "Yeah, she really is something special."

Fiza teased me endlessly, asking about our relationship, our future, and everything in between. It was nice to share my feelings with someone who genuinely cared, but I couldn't shake the feeling that something was off. Maybe it was just the distance, but a part of me felt uneasy.

Two days later, as I was packing to return to the hostel, my phone rang. It was Siddhart. His voice was tense, laced with an urgency that immediately set off alarm bells in my mind. "Fawaz, man, you need to know something. It's about Zoya."

My heart skipped a beat. "What happened? Is she okay?"

There was a brief pause before Siddhart continued, "She's okay now, but Ayush… that bastard tried to get close to her. He asked her out, and when she said no, he wouldn't back off. He grabbed her, Fawaz. He fucking touched her."

Rage exploded inside me, white-hot and uncontrollable. I clenched my fists so tightly that my knuckles turned white. "What the hell did he do to her?"

Siddhart tried to calm me down. "Azal and I were there. We saw it happen and stepped in before it got worse. We got Zoya away from him and took her back to the hostel. But she was shaken up, man. Really shaken up."

Hearing that made my blood boil even more. I could barely see straight through the fury. "I swear to God, Siddhart, I'm going to kill that piece of shit. How dare he touch her?"

"Fawaz, listen," Siddhart said firmly, "Zoya doesn't want you to fight him. She's already upset, and she doesn't want you getting into trouble because of this."

I was seething, pacing back and forth in my room. "I don't care what happens to me. He doesn't get to put his hands on her. Not him, not anyone."

"I get it, Fawaz, but Zoya's been through enough already. She needs you to be there for her, not to throw punches. Can you promise me you won't do anything stupid?"

I hesitated, my mind racing with images of Ayush's smug face and the way Zoya must have felt in that moment—helpless, scared, alone. But I knew Siddhart was right. I couldn't make things worse for her. "I'll try, man. But if I see him, I can't make any guarantees."

After I hung up with Siddhart, I immediately called Zoya. My hands were shaking as I waited for her to pick up. When she finally answered, her voice was steady, but I could hear the strain behind it. "Hello?"

"Zoya, what did that son of a bitch do to you?" My voice was raw with anger.

There was a pause, and then she replied, her tone careful, almost too calm. "Fawaz, it's okay. He just asked me out, that's all."

I could tell she was trying to downplay it, trying to protect me from the truth. But I wasn't buying it. "Zoya, don't lie to me. Siddhart told me everything. He touched you, didn't he?"

She sighed, and I could hear the weariness in her voice. "Yes, he did. But I handled it. Azal and Siddhart were there, and they helped me. It's over now."

My chest tightened with a mixture of fury and helplessness. "Zoya, I swear to God, if I were there—"

"Please, Fawaz," she interrupted, her voice cracking slightly, "I don't want you to fight him. I don't want this to escalate. I just… I just want to move on from it."

I was silent for a moment, trying to rein in the anger that was threatening to consume me. I could hear the pain in her voice, the way she was struggling to keep it together. It broke my heart that I wasn't there to protect her when she needed me the most.

"I promise I won't do anything," I finally said, though the words felt like a lie even as I spoke them. "But if he ever tries something like that again…"

"He won't," she said softly. "I'll make sure of it."

We talked for a while longer, and though she tried to sound strong, I could tell that what happened had affected her deeply. When we finally hung up, I was left with a sense of helplessness that I wasn't used to. I had always thought I could protect her, but this time, I had been miles away while she faced that creep on her own.

As I lay in bed that night, staring at the ceiling, I couldn't shake the image of Ayush grabbing her, of the fear she must have felt. My fists throbbed where I had punched the wall earlier, but the physical pain was nothing compared to the torment in my heart.

I knew that Zoya wanted to forget about it, to move on, but I wasn't sure if I could. The promise I made to her felt like a weight around my neck, and I wasn't sure how long I could carry it without breaking.

All I knew was that when I got back to the hostel, I needed to be there for her—really be there. Because if there was one thing I couldn't stand, it was the thought of her being hurt and me being powerless to stop it.

Chapter-25

When I returned to the hostel, I was greeted by the familiar faces of my friends, and though the cloud of what had happened with Zoya still hung over me, their presence was a welcome distraction.

Azal was the first to spot me, a grin spreading across his face as he called out, "Look who finally decided to grace us with his presence! How's the family, dude?"

I managed a smile, though my mind was still racing. "Everything's fine now. Just glad to be back."

Aryan clapped me on the back. "Good to have you back, man. We were starting to think you might've forgotten about us."

"Forgotten? Nah, I could never forget you idiots," I joked, trying to ease the tension that still gnawed at me.

Siddhart joined in, pretending to be hurt. "Forgot us? After all the drama we have lined up for you? Never!"

We laughed, and for a moment, the weight on my chest lifted. But deep down, I knew it was only a matter of time before the unresolved anger would surface again. We spent the evening catching up, cracking jokes, and teasing each other about everything from Azal's mysterious poetry sessions to Aryan's latest gym routine.

The next day, I headed to class, the familiar sights and sounds of campus doing little to quell the storm inside me. My anger toward Ayush simmered beneath the surface, but I was determined to keep my promise to Zoya. No matter how much I wanted to, I couldn't let myself lose control.

During the break, I went to the washroom, trying to clear my head. But when I returned to class, the sight that greeted me made my blood run cold. Zoya was standing near her desk, talking to Ayush. The sight of them together, of him daring to speak to her after what he had done, snapped something inside me.

Without thinking, I charged toward him, my vision narrowing to nothing but his face. Before anyone could react, I swung my fist and punched him hard, right in the face. Ayush staggered back, clutching his nose as blood started to flow. But that wasn't enough. I pushed him, sending him crashing to the floor, and then I was on him, my fists pounding into him again and again.

"Do you know what she's going through? Do you know what happened to her, you piece of shit?" I snarled, the words spilling out of me as I continued to hit him. I didn't care who was watching. All I could see was red.

The sounds around me—the gasps, the shouts—were muffled, distant, like I was underwater. It wasn't until I heard Zoya scream my name that I stopped. Her voice cut through the haze of anger, pulling me back to reality.

I looked up to see her standing there, her face a mask of shock and horror. And then, before I could react, she stepped forward and slapped me, hard, across the face. The sting of it jolted me back to my senses.

"He only came to apologize to me," she said, her voice trembling with anger and disbelief. Her words hit me like a ton of bricks, and I realized with dawning horror what I had done.

Zoya turned and walked out of the classroom, leaving me standing there, stunned and humiliated. The room was dead silent, all eyes on me as the reality of my actions sank in.

I tried calling Zoya multiple times that day, but she didn't pick up. My messages went unanswered. I spent the rest of the day in a daze, barely registering what was happening around me. The next three classes were a blur, my mind consumed with worry and regret.

That evening, at the girls' hostel, Riya, Preeti, and Sneha were talking about what had happened. Zoya sat with them, silent and withdrawn, her face pale. They knew why I had reacted the way I did—they knew I thought Ayush was harassing her again—but they were still angry. I could see it in their eyes, in the way they exchanged glances when Zoya finally spoke up.

"He was just apologizing," Zoya said quietly, her voice devoid of emotion. "He didn't deserve what happened."

Back at the boys' hostel, I sat on the balcony with Azal and Aryan, the cool evening air doing little to soothe the turmoil inside me. I couldn't stop thinking about Zoya—about how I had broken my promise to her, how I had let my anger control me. I felt like I had failed her in the worst possible way.

Azal, ever perceptive, noticed the tension in my shoulders, the way I was staring out into the distance with a clenched jaw. Without a word, he reached into his pocket, pulled out a cigarette, and handed it to me.

I looked at him, feeling a mix of anger and gratitude. "Seriously, Azal?"

He shrugged, lighting one for himself. "Just take it, Fawaz. Thank me later."

I hesitated for a moment before taking it from him. The first puff was harsh, burning my throat, but the second was better. By the third, I could feel the edge of my anxiety dulling, the tension easing just a little.

But as the cigarette burned down to the filter, the weight of my actions settled back on my shoulders. I wasn't happy with myself—for breaking my promise, for letting my anger get the better of me, for pushing Zoya further away.

The next four days were torture. Zoya ignored me completely, her absence like a constant ache in my chest. She hung out with the girls, avoiding me at every turn. I tried to talk to her, to apologize, but she wouldn't give me the chance. It was like she had built a wall around herself, and I was on the outside, powerless to reach her.

Each day that passed without hearing her voice, without seeing her smile, felt like a lifetime. My friends tried to distract me, pulling me into conversations and jokes, but nothing could shake the feeling that I had ruined everything. The laughter and camaraderie that usually brought me comfort now felt hollow, a stark contrast to the turmoil in my heart.

I knew I had to make things right, but I didn't know how. All I could do was wait and hope that Zoya would forgive me, that she would understand why I did what I did, even if I couldn't fully understand it myself.

Chapter-26

The days without Zoya were agonizing. Every moment felt like a wound that wouldn't heal, a reminder of how badly I had screwed up. The laughter and camaraderie that once filled our group now seemed distant, as if I were merely a shadow of my former self. I avoided eye contact with my friends, ashamed of the person I'd become. My thoughts constantly circled back to Zoya, replaying the moment she slapped me, her eyes filled with hurt and disappointment. It was a memory that haunted me, a pain sharper than any physical blow.

My friends tried their best to support me, but there was a palpable tension in the air. They knew why I'd reacted the way I did, but they couldn't condone the violence, especially not after the promise I had made to Zoya. They could see the guilt eating away at me, but none of them had the answer I was desperately seeking: How could I fix this? How could I make Zoya forgive me?

On the fifth day, something in me snapped. The weight of Zoya's silence, the distance between us—it was all too much. I couldn't go on like this, not knowing if I'd lost her forever. I needed to do something, anything, to show her how much she meant to me.

That night, I found myself in the common room of the boys' hostel, staring blankly at the wall as Aryan, Azal, Abad, and

Siddhart sat around me. The usual banter was absent, replaced by an uncomfortable quiet. Finally, Azal broke the silence.

"Fawaz, this isn't you," he said, his voice low but firm. "You can't just sit here and let this tear you apart."

"I don't know what else to do," I replied, my voice hollow. "She won't even look at me, Azal. I've lost her."

"You haven't lost her yet," Aryan interjected, leaning forward. "But you will if you don't do something. She needs to see how much you care, how much you regret what happened."

The idea hit me then, like a spark in the darkness. It wasn't grand or elaborate, but it was genuine—it was me. I looked up at my friends, a glimmer of hope returning to my eyes. "I think I know what to do," I said, my voice gaining strength. "But I'll need your help."

The next morning, I woke up early, the plan I'd concocted the night before burning in my mind. I texted Zoya, asking her to meet me outside her hostel. I knew it was a long shot, but I had to try. To my surprise, she agreed, though her response was curt, devoid of the warmth that once colored our conversations.

As I stood outside, waiting, my heart pounded in my chest. Every second felt like an eternity. Finally, I saw her emerging from the hostel, her expression guarded. She stopped a few feet away from me, crossing her arms.

"What do you want, Fawaz?" she asked, her tone cold, though I could see the flicker of pain in her eyes.

"Just... please come with me," I said, trying to keep my voice steady. "I need to show you something."

She hesitated, clearly torn between anger and curiosity, but finally, she nodded. I led her around the side of the building, to the small garden where we had spent so much time together. It was a place filled with memories—good ones, ones I hoped she hadn't forgotten.

As we turned the corner, Zoya froze. Her eyes widened as she took in the sight before her. My friends were there, holding up a large banner we had stayed up all night making. It read, "I'm s orry, Zoya," but it wasn't just an apology—it was a collage of memories, snapshots of our time together. Each picture, each moment, was a testament to what we had shared, what I had almost thrown away.

Aryan started playing the guitar, the soft melody of our favorite song filling the air. It was the song we used to listen to on lazy afternoons, the one that always made her smile. I stepped in front of her, my heart in my throat, and began to speak, my voice shaking.

"Zoya, I know I've hurt you," I began, forcing myself to meet her gaze. "I let my anger take over, and I made a terrible mistake. But it wasn't just the violence, it was the fact that I didn't trust you to handle things on your own. I broke my promise to you, and I'm so sorry. I've spent the last few days thinking about what I did, about how I let you down. And I can't bear the thought of losing you because of my own stupidity."

Her expression softened, though she didn't speak. I continued, my voice thick with emotion. "These past few days without you have been the worst of my life. I didn't realize just how much you mean to me until you weren't there anymore. Zoya, I'm not asking for you to forgive me right away, but please, just give me a chance to make it right."

A tear slid down her cheek, and she quickly wiped it away, trying to maintain her composure. The sight of her crying because of me—it was like a knife to my heart. I took a deep breath, my own eyes stinging with unshed tears.

"I love you, Zoya," I whispered, my voice breaking. "I love you more than anything, and I'll do whatever it takes to prove that to you. Just... don't shut me out."

There was a long silence, the only sound being the soft strumming of Aryan's guitar. Zoya looked down, her emotions warring on her face. Then, slowly, she took a step toward me, her eyes meeting mine with a vulnerability that made my chest tighten.

"You're such an idiot, Fawaz," she said softly, her voice trembling. "But I can't stay mad at you forever."

My heart soared at her words, but I didn't move, afraid that any sudden action might break the fragile moment we were sharing. Zoya reached out, her hand trembling as she touched my face, her fingers brushing against my cheek.

"I was so angry," she continued, her voice barely above a whisper. "Angry that you didn't trust me, angry that you broke your promise. But I also know why you did it. You were trying to protect me, even if you went about it the wrong way."

I nodded, swallowing hard. "I never wanted to hurt you, Zoya. I just... I saw him with you, and I lost it. I couldn't stand the thought of him hurting you again."

"I know," she replied, her voice softening even more. "And that's why I'm willing to give you another chance. But, Fawaz, you have to promise me—really promise me—that you'll think before you act next time. Trust me to handle things on my own."

"I promise," I said, my voice thick with emotion. "I'll do better, Zoya. I swear."

For a moment, we just stood there, the weight of the past few days hanging between us. Then, without warning, Zoya stepped forward and wrapped her arms around me, burying her face in my chest. I held her tightly, feeling the tension melt away as she clung to me.

"I missed you so much," she whispered, her voice muffled against my shirt.

"I missed you too," I murmured, pressing a kiss to the top of her head. "I was so scared I'd lost you."

She pulled back slightly, looking up at me with tear-filled eyes. "You didn't lose me, Fawaz. But you came close. Don't ever do that to me again."

"I won't," I promised, brushing a tear from her cheek. "I love you too much to ever risk losing you again."

She smiled then, a real smile that lit up her entire face. It was the first time I'd seen her smile in days, and it felt like the sun breaking through a stormy sky. I leaned down, pressing a gentle kiss to her forehead, and she closed her eyes, leaning into me.

We stood there for a long time, wrapped in each other's arms, while our friends looked on, relieved smiles on their faces. The tension that had hung over us for days finally began to dissipate, replaced by a sense of hope and renewal.

As we walked back to class together, hand in hand, I knew that things wouldn't be easy. We still had a lot to work through, a lot of trust to rebuild. But for the first time in days, I felt like we could make it through—together. And that was all that mattered.

Chapter- 27

The campus buzzed with excitement as the annual inter-college cultural fest approached. Zoya and I were immersed in the chaos of organizing the event, and despite the stress, there was a palpable sense of camaraderie between us. We spent countless hours together in the library, working side by side on the preparations, and I felt that our bond was growing stronger.

One evening, as we were wrapping up our planning session, a new presence on campus made itself known. Arjun, a senior from the third year and the head of the Debate Society, had recently joined our college by parallel admission. Known for his eloquence and sharp wit, Arjun quickly became a prominent figure on campus. His reputation preceded him, and his arrival sparked interest and admiration among many students, including those in the Debate Society, where Zoya was an active member.

It was during a meeting for the fest that Arjun first made his move. He approached our table, his demeanor confident and poised. "Hey, Zoya," he said with a charming smile. "I hear you're heavily involved in the fest preparations. If there's anything I can do to help, just let me know."

Zoya looked up, a bit surprised but grateful. "Thanks, Arjun. We've got most things covered, but we appreciate the offer."

Arjun's presence became increasingly noticeable. He started showing up at various meetings and events related to the fest, often offering unsolicited advice and suggestions. His charisma and intelligence were undeniable, and he quickly became a favorite among the students. I couldn't help but notice that he was particularly attentive to Zoya, frequently engaging her in conversation and praising her work.

As days passed, Arjun's interactions with Zoya grew more frequent. It seemed as though he had a knack for showing up whenever Zoya and I were working together. His comments were always carefully measured, a mix of praise and flirtation that seemed designed to keep her attention. Despite my attempts to stay composed, I found myself growing increasingly uneasy. Each time he complimented Zoya's work or touched her arm slightly as he spoke, a surge of jealousy twisted in my chest.

The day of the fest arrived, and the excitement on campus was palpable. Zoya and I worked tirelessly to ensure everything went smoothly. Arjun, as expected, was deeply involved in the event. His role as the head of the Debate Society made him a significant presence, and his ability to navigate the complexities of the fest was impressive. Yet, it was his closeness with Zoya that unsettled me.

During one of the quieter moments of the fest, I saw Arjun and Zoya deep in conversation near the debate stage. They seemed engrossed in an animated discussion, their proximity too intimate for my comfort. My heart sank as I watched them laugh and lean closer, their bodies almost touching. The scene felt like a punch to the gut.

Later that evening, I couldn't hold back my frustration any longer. "Zoya, I need to talk to you about Arjun," I said, my voice trembling as I pulled her aside. I could feel the weight of my jealousy pressing down on me, making it hard to speak calmly.

Zoya looked at me with a mixture of surprise and concern. "What's wrong, Fawaz?"

"I've noticed how often he's around you and how close he's been getting. It feels like he's trying to undermine what we have," I said, trying to keep my tone steady but failing as my emotions broke through.

Zoya's expression softened as she reached out to me. "Fawaz, Arjun is just being supportive. He's a senior and the head of the Debate Society—he's trying to make things easier for us. There's nothing more to it."

I wasn't entirely convinced. "It just feels like he's more interested in you than in helping with the fest. Every time he's around, I feel like I'm losing you."

Zoya sighed, her eyes reflecting a deep sadness. "Arjun's advice is valuable, Fawaz. He's been in this field for a long time. But I'm here with you, and that's what matters."

Despite her reassurances, I couldn't shake the feeling that Arjun was a significant threat. His status and influence made him a formidable rival, and I was worried that his presence might overshadow our relationship. The more I tried to push away my insecurities, the more they seemed to intensify.

The days following the fest were filled with tension. Arjun continued to be a frequent presence in our lives, and his interactions with Zoya remained close. I struggled to keep my emotions in check, grappling with feelings of jealousy and insecurity. Every time Zoya mentioned Arjun or talked about their conversations, a pang of resentment flared up inside me.

One evening, as we were winding down after a particularly hectic day, I saw Zoya and Arjun talking animatedly near the Debate Society's office. They were laughing and sharing a moment that felt more personal than professional. My heart ached, and I fought the urge to confront Zoya again.

That night, as I lay in bed, the jealousy gnawed at me. I replayed every interaction between Zoya and Arjun in my mind, each memory adding to my frustration. I knew that my feelings were affecting my relationship with Zoya, but I couldn't seem to control them.

The next day, Zoya approached me, her eyes filled with concern. "Fawaz, I know things have been tense between us lately. I want you to know that I'm here for you and that I care about us."

I looked at her, my heart heavy. "I know, Zoya. It's just hard for me to see Arjun around you so much. I can't help but feel like he's a threat to what we have."

Zoya reached out and took my hand. "Arjun is a part of our college life now, but that doesn't change how I feel about you. I need you to trust me, Fawaz."

As I looked into her eyes, I realized that my insecurities were clouding my judgment. I needed to address my feelings and trust Zoya, or risk losing her to my own fears. The challenge of dealing with Arjun was more than just a test of our relationship; it was a test of my own ability to handle insecurities and trust.

The tension between Zoya and me simmered as the fest came to a close. Arjun's presence and his close interactions with Zoya had taken a toll on me, but I tried to push my feelings aside and focus on our relationship.

One evening, as I was heading back to my hostel, I saw Zoya and Arjun talking near the Debate Society office. They were engrossed in conversation, their laughter mingling with the cool night air. My heart sank as I approached them, feeling a familiar surge of jealousy.

“Hey, Zoya,” I greeted, trying to sound casual despite the knots in my stomach.

Zoya looked up, her smile faltering slightly when she saw my expression. “Hey, Fawaz. We were just discussing some ideas for the debate team.”

Arjun, sensing the tension, stepped in with a smile. “Well, Zoya, it’s been great catching up. I was actually wondering if you’d be interested in joining me for dinner tomorrow. It’s a celebration for the success of the fest.”

Zoya glanced at me, her eyes searching for a reaction. “That sounds nice, Arjun. But I’m not sure if I’ll be free.”

Arjun didn’t miss a beat. “No worries. Just let me know. I’d love to have you there.”

As Arjun walked away, I could feel the weight of his offer hanging in the air. I waited until he was out of sight before turning to Zoya. “So, what’s going on with that dinner invitation?”

Zoya sighed, her expression pensive. “It’s just dinner , Fawaz. Arjun’s trying to be supportive and celebrate the success of the fest. It doesn’t mean anything.”

I tried to mask my frustration. “But it’s not just dinner, is it? I’ve seen the way he looks at you. He’s making a move.”

Zoya’s eyes softened, and she reached out to take my hand. “Fawaz, I understand how you’re feeling, but you have to trust me. Arjun’s a senior and a friend. There’s nothing more to it.”

Despite her reassurance, I couldn't shake the unease. The next day, as Zoya prepared for the dinner with Arjun, I found it hard to concentrate on anything else. My mind was consumed with thoughts of them together, and the insecurity gnawed at me.

That evening, I decided to follow them discreetly. I wanted to see what was happening and to understand if my fears were justified. As Zoya and Arjun left for dinner, I trailed behind, careful to stay out of sight.

They arrived at a cozy restaurant not far from campus, a place with dim lighting and an intimate atmosphere. From my vantage point across the street, I watched as they were seated at a table near the window. Arjun pulled out Zoya's chair, and they settled into their seats, engaging in conversation.

I could see Arjun leaning in slightly, his gestures and expressions indicating a level of familiarity and flirtation. Zoya, while polite and engaged, appeared somewhat reserved. The sight of them together, sharing a meal and laughing, only fueled my anxiety.

After what felt like an eternity, I decided I couldn't take it anymore. I walked back to the hostel, my mind racing with conflicting emotions.

Chapter-28

Hours later, as I was lost in thought, I noticed a missed call from Zoya and a text message that read, "Please come to the gate. I need you."

My heart raced with panic. I hurried back to the hostel, my thoughts a jumble of worry and fear. When I reached the gate, Zoya was waiting for me, her face tear-streaked and pale. Seeing her in such distress felt like a punch to the gut.

"Zoya!" I rushed to her, pulling her into a tight embrace. Her sobs were muffled against my chest. "What happened? Are you okay?"

Through her tears, she managed to speak, her voice trembling with anguish. "I thought I could trust him. I was wrong, Fawaz. He… he tried to… I'm so sorry I didn't listen to you."

Her words were barely coherent, but the pain in her voice was unmistakable. I could feel a surge of rage building inside me. The thought of Arjun's betrayal ignited a burning fury. I wanted to confront him, to make him pay for what he had done. But I remembered my promise to Zoya about avoiding violence and fought to control my anger.

"Come on," I said, trying to keep my voice steady despite the storm of emotions inside me. "We need to talk."

I led her to the MBA garden, a quiet spot where we could escape the noise and chaos. The cool night air was a stark contrast to the heated turmoil we had just experienced. We found a secluded bench under the soft glow of the moonlight, the silence between us heavy with unspoken words.

Zoya took a deep breath, trying to steady her emotions. "Arjun took me to an ice cream parlor after dinner," she began, her voice barely above a whisper. "I was hesitant, but he insisted. We were eating, and then he touched my chin to wipe off a drop of ice cream. His touch felt wrong. And then, he leaned in to kiss me."

Her words were a raw wound, and my heart ached with every syllable. The image of Arjun's attempted advance was like a knife twisting in my chest. I fought to stay composed, to offer her the support she needed.

"What did you do?" I asked, my voice strained with the effort to keep calm.

"I slapped him," Zoya said, her voice breaking. "I couldn't believe what was happening. I ran out of the parlor, and I just needed to get back here. I was so scared, Fawaz. I didn't know what to do."

My anger flared again, and I felt a primal urge to seek out Arjun. But I took a deep breath, reminding myself of my promise. Instead, I focused on comforting Zoya.

"You did the right thing by standing up for yourself," I said gently. "I'm so sorry you had to go through that. You're strong, Zoya, and you didn't deserve any of this."

Zoya looked up at me, her eyes filled with regret and fear. "I should have trusted you, Fawaz. I should have been more careful about who I let in."

I shook my head, trying to offer reassurance. "It's not your fault. Sometimes people seem trustworthy, but their true intentions only become clear later. The important thing is that you're safe now, and we'll get through this together."

We sat in silence for a while, the weight of the night's events pressing heavily on us. As I listened to Zoya, I realized that my own insecurities had clouded my judgment. The challenge was not just dealing with Arjun but also confronting my own fears and learning to trust Zoya.

"I'm sorry for how I reacted," I said quietly. "I know my jealousy got the best of me. I just wanted to protect you, but I see now that I need to work on my own trust issues."

Zoya squeezed my hand, her touch warm and comforting. "It's okay, Fawaz. We'll figure this out together. We need to trust each other and be honest about our feelings."

As the night wore on, we talked about how to navigate the complexities of our emotions and relationships. The conversation was painful but healing, offering a sense of clarity amidst the turmoil. We both knew that our bond had been tested, but facing these challenges together made us stronger.

Chapter-29

After some time, my phone buzzed with a message. It was Siddhart.

Siddhart: "Heard what happened. Where are you? Let's deal with this."

I stared at the message, my thumb hovering over the keyboard. Siddhart was the last person I expected to hear from. He was always the one who would escalate situations rather than de-escalate them. And right now, I wasn't sure that was what Zoya needed.

But before I could respond, Siddhart's name flashed on my screen again. This time, it was a call. Zoya looked up at me, sensing the change in my demeanor.

"Who is it?" she asked, her voice still shaky.

"It's Siddhart," I said, answering the call. "He wants to help."

"Yo, man, where are you? Let's go find this guy and teach him a lesson," Siddhart's voice was all fire and brimstone, just as I'd expected.

"Not now, Sid," I said, trying to keep my voice calm, even though I was feeling anything but. "Zoya's been through enough tonight. She doesn't need more violence."

"What are you talking about? This guy crossed a line. We can't just let him get away with it," Siddhart shot back, incredulous.

Zoya's eyes were wide as she listened to the exchange, her grip on my hand tightening. She was afraid, not just of Arjun, but of what might happen next.

"Siddhart, I promised Zoya I wouldn't resort to violence," I said, struggling to keep my voice steady. "I'm not going to break that promise, no matter how much I want to. We need to handle this differently."

There was a long pause on the other end of the line. When Siddhart spoke again, his voice was low, almost cold. "So, you're just going to let this slide? Let him walk around like nothing happened?"

"No, of course not," I snapped, frustration bubbling to the surface. "But fighting him won't change anything. It'll only make things worse. We need to think this through."

Zoya looked at me, her eyes filled with gratitude, but also a hint of fear. Fear that Siddhart might not understand, that he might take matters into his own hands regardless of what I said.

"Fine," Siddhart said finally, his tone laced with disappointment. "But don't expect me to just stand by and do nothing. This guy needs to be taught a lesson."

"I'm not asking you to do nothing, Sid," I said, trying to reach a middle ground. "But we have to be smart about this. We can talk to someone in authority, report him. There are other ways."

"Yeah, sure, whatever you say," Siddhart replied, but the edge in his voice told me he wasn't convinced. Before I could say more, he hung up.

I let out a frustrated sigh, feeling the weight of the situation pressing down on me. I'd always relied on Siddhart to have my back, but now it felt like we were on opposite sides of a line I hadn't even realized we'd drawn.

Zoya looked up at me, her expression torn. "I'm sorry," she whispered. "I didn't mean to cause a rift between you and Siddhart."

"Don't be sorry," I said, shaking my head. "This isn't your fault. Sid just… he deals with things differently. But we'll figure it out."

The rest of the night passed in a blur. Zoya and I talked for hours in the MBA garden, discussing everything from what had happened with Arjun to how she could protect herself moving forward. But no matter how much we talked, there was an undercurrent of tension that neither of us could ignore.

When I finally walked her back to the hostel, she seemed more at peace, but I couldn't say the same for myself. As I turned to leave, she stopped me, her hand resting on my arm.

"Thank you," she said softly. "For being there for me. For not letting anger control you."

I gave her a small smile, though it didn't reach my eyes. "I'll always be here for you, Zoya. No matter what."

"Zoya," I said quietly, after a long pause, "I need you to promise me something too."

She looked at me, her eyes questioning. "What is it?"

"If anything like this ever happens again," I began, my voice trembling slightly with the effort to stay calm, "if anyone ever tries to hurt you again… tell me. Don't try to handle it alone. Let me be there for you."

"I will," she said softly, her fingers tightening around mine. "I promise."

By the time I walked her back to the hostel, it was well past midnight. She seemed calmer, more composed, but I could still see the hurt in her eyes. It broke me a little more each time I saw it.

"Thank you," she said quietly, as we stood at the gate. "For being there. For not letting your anger take over."

I managed a small smile, though it felt forced. "You don't have to thank me for that. I'd do anything for you, Zoya."

She nodded, but her expression was still troubled. "What about Siddhart? He's… he's not going to cause any trouble, is he?"

The mention of Siddhart brought back the tension I'd tried to bury. He was still a wild card in all this, and I wasn't sure how to handle him.

"I'll talk to him," I promised. "He won't do anything without talking to me first."

"Okay," she said, though I could see the doubt in her eyes. "Just… be careful. I don't want this to get worse."

"I will," I assured her, even though I wasn't entirely sure how. "Get some rest, okay? We'll figure everything out tomorrow."

As she turned to head inside, I watched her go, a heavy feeling settling in my chest. I knew this wasn't over—not by a long shot. The anger inside me was still there, simmering just below the surface, and I wasn't sure how long I could keep it in check.

I made my way back to my room, my thoughts a tangled mess of frustration, guilt, and anger. I'd done what I could to be there for Zoya, but it didn't feel like enough. Not when Arjun was still out there, probably laughing about what he'd done, thinking he'd gotten away with it.

When I finally got back to my room, the first thing I did was call Siddhart. He answered on the second ring, his voice gruff with sleep.

"What's up, man? Did you talk to Zoya?"

"Yeah," I said, struggling to keep my voice even. "She's... she's okay, but she's shaken up. Look, Siddhart, I need you to promise me something."

"What's that?" he asked, his tone cautious.

"Promise me you won't go after Arjun," I said, the words burning in my throat. "I know you want to, but we need to be smart about this. We can't just... we can't just start a fight."

There was a long silence on the other end of the line. When Siddhart finally spoke, his voice was hard. "So, what are we supposed to do? Just let him get away with it?"

"No," I said quickly. "But we need to handle this the right way. Zoya's been through enough. We can't make things worse for her."

"And what if the right way doesn't work?" Siddhart shot back. "What if he just laughs in our faces?"

"Then we'll deal with it." I replied.

Chapter-30

The day had begun with an ominous tension that hung in the air, thick and suffocating, as though the world knew what was coming. Ever since Zoya confided in me about Arjun's actions, I couldn't shake the fury that coursed through me. I wanted to protect her, to shield her from the pain she'd experienced, and make sure Arjun paid for what he did. I wasn't alone in this resolve; Siddhart shared my anger, and together we decided to take matters into our own hands.

Our plan was simple but direct.we would confront Arjun's girlfriend, Neha, and tell her the truth about him. She deserved to know the kind of person he was, the way he had tried to manipulate Zoya. It wasn't an easy conversation….Neha had always trusted Arjun, and shattering that trust felt almost cruel. But she had the right to know, and when we finally told her, the devastation in her eyes was like a mirror of our own pain.

Neha's tears flowed freely as she absorbed our words, but her sorrow quickly turned to determination. She broke things off with Arjun without hesitation, her voice steady despite the quiver of heartbreak underlying each word. We thought that would be the end of it….a harsh but necessary conclusion to a painful chapter. But deep down, we knew Arjun wouldn't let it go.

The afternoon sun was dipping low when I met Zoya outside the classroom. The golden light softened her features, casting a warm glow on her face. For a moment, it was just us, and the world seemed at peace. She was smiling, that small, comforting smile that always made my heart feel lighter, but it didn't last.

Out of nowhere, a rough hand seized my collar, yanking me backward with a force that nearly knocked the breath out of me. I barely had time to register what was happening before a stinging slap landed on my cheek, the force of it turning my head sharply to the side. The world spun slightly from the impact, and a second slap followed before I could even react. My skin burned, and a dull ache spread through my jaw.

The pain was disorienting, but what hit me harder was the realization of who was behind it. I was face-to-face with a group of Arjun's friends, their expressions twisted with malicious glee. And there, standing just behind them, was Arjun himself, his eyes blazing with fury. "You thought you could humiliate me and walk away?" he spat, his voice venomous. His gaze flicked to Zoya, standing frozen beside me. "And you," he snarled, his voice dripping with contempt, "you're nothing but a bitch for running away from me like that and for who ... .this freshy scumbag."

The word hit like a punch to the gut, and I felt a surge of protective rage rise up inside me, hot and uncontrollable. My hands clenched into fists, every instinct screaming at me to fight back, to wipe that smirk off Arjun's face. But before I could do anything, Aryan appeared from the crowd. His face was a mask of fury as he lunged at the guy who had slapped me, his fist connecting with a sickening crunch that echoed in the courtyard. Blood spurted from the guy's nose, and he stumbled back, shock written all over his face.

That one punch was the spark that set off an explosion. Siddhart, Azal, and Abad were instantly at my side, and suddenly, we were in the midst of a full-blown brawl. It was chaos....fists flying, bodies colliding, shouts and curses filling the air. My mind was a blur of adrenaline and pain, but the only thing I could think about was Zoya. I had to protect her. I had to keep her safe.

But in the middle of the fight, there was no clear way to do that. All I could do was swing and dodge, trying to fend off the blows coming from all sides. My knuckles ached with every punch, but I barely noticed. The only thing that mattered was not letting them hurt her.

The girls—Zoya, Preeti, Sneha, and Riya—stood off to the side, their faces pale with fear. They looked so small and helpless, caught in the storm of violence that had erupted around them. I could see the terror in Zoya's eyes, the way her hands trembled as she watched us, and it broke my heart. This wasn't what I wanted. I had promised her I wouldn't let my anger control me, and here I was, doing exactly that.

Then, as suddenly as it had started, the fight was over. A teacher stormed into the scene, his voice booming with authority as he wrenched us apart. "Enough!" he roared, his eyes blazing with fury as he surveyed the chaos. He took in the sight of us—bruised, bloodied, and breathing hard—but it was Arjun and his friends who bore the full brunt of his wrath. "You started this," the teacher growled, his voice like ice. "Report to the dean's office immediately. You're all suspended."

Arjun's face twisted with barely suppressed rage, but he didn't dare argue. He shot me one last venomous look before stalking off, his friends trailing behind him, still clutching their injuries.

As the adrenaline began to fade, the pain in my jaw and knuckles became more pronounced. But it was nothing compared to the guilt gnawing at my insides. I had failed Zoya, broken my promise to her. The realization hit me like a punch to the gut. I couldn't bear to look at her, not after what I'd done.

The walk back to the hostel was heavy with silence. The girls took us back to our rooms, tending to our injuries with soft hands and even softer words. But I couldn't focus on anything they were saying. My thoughts were consumed with Zoya—what she must be thinking, how disappointed she must be in me.

But when I finally mustered the courage to look up at her, what I saw in her eyes wasn't anger or disappointment. Instead, there was a deep understanding, a kind of acceptance that I hadn't expected. She wasn't mad. In fact, she seemed more concerned about me than anything else. Her hands were gentle as she cleaned the cut on my cheek, her touch so careful it was almost tender.

The evening passed in a haze of antiseptic and whispered reassurances, but I couldn't shake the feeling that I had let her down. When everyone else finally left, leaving me alone with Zoya, the weight of what had happened pressed down on me like a physical burden.

"Zoya," I said, my voice low and rough from the emotions I had been holding back all day. "I need to tell you something… something I've never told anyone before."

She looked at me, her eyes full of concern and something else—something that looked a lot like love. She nodded, urging me to continue.

"When I was in 5th standard," I began, my voice trembling despite my best efforts to keep it steady, "I was bullied. Every day, for a whole year, I was tormented by my classmates. They took my money, pushed me around, called me names… I was just a kid, and I didn't know how to make it stop. I was too scared to tell anyone. I thought… I thought it would make me look weak."

The words spilled out of me, each one dragging up memories I had tried so hard to bury. My throat tightened as I spoke, the pain of those old wounds still fresh despite the years that had passed. Tears pricked at the corners of my eyes, but I blinked them back, focusing on the warmth of Zoya's hand in mine. Her touch was grounding, giving me the strength to continue.

"One day, my parents noticed the bruises. My dad was so angry… he came to the school and confronted the teacher in front of the whole class. They got into a shouting match, and it was the most humiliating moment of my life. We left the school that day, and I never went back. But after that… My dad taught me how to fight back. He told me to never let anyone bully me again. And I haven't… but sometimes, I wonder if I've gone too far."

My voice cracked as I finished, the weight of those memories pressing down on me. I had never told anyone about this, not even Siddhart or Abad or anyone. But with Zoya, it felt like a burden I could finally lay down.

Zoya's eyes shimmered with tears as she listened, her hand squeezing mine as if trying to transfer some of her strength to me. When I finished, she pulled me into her arms, holding me close. I buried my face in her shoulder, the tears I had been holding back finally breaking free.

"I'm so sorry you went through that," she whispered, her voice thick with emotion. "But you're not that scared little boy anymore. You're strong, and you've fought for yourself and for others. But you don't have to fight alone, not anymore. I'm here for you, and I'll always be here, no matter what."

Her words, so full of love and compassion, cut through the walls I had built around myself. For the first time in a long time,

I allowed myself to be vulnerable, to let someone else carry some of the weight I had been bearing alone for so long.

"I love you, Zoya," I whispered, my voice breaking with the intensity of my emotions. "I don't know what I'd do without you."

She pulled back just enough to look into my eyes, her own shimmering with tears. "I love you too, my Batman ."

Chapter-31

For a few days everything seemed normal. Zoya and I were thriving and acing every exam because we studied together everyday in the library. Few days after the exams were over, one night she called me. Her voice was frantic, breaking through the static on my phone. "Fawaz, I need to go back home. There's an emergency." Her words were rushed, filled with a fear I had never heard from her before.

"What's wrong?" I asked, trying to keep my voice steady despite the panic rising in my chest.

"It's Farida and Rauf. They're trying to sell Dad's company, and they need my signature. I don't want to sell it—I want to run it myself once I graduate. But they're making it impossible." She hesitated, the line crackling with her distress. "I'm leaving now. I can't talk much longer."

I wanted to go with her, to offer my support and comfort, but she insisted that she needed to face this alone. "Please, Fawaz. I need to do this on my own."

Two days later, I paced the hostel, unable to shake the worry gnawing at me. Zoya hadn't returned my calls or texts. Each unanswered message felt like a hammer striking my chest. When a month had passed with no word, my anxiety turned to dread.

In college, the news of Zoya's disappearance spread like wildfire. The group—Abad, Siddhart, Riya, Preeti, Sneha, Aryan and Azal—gathered, their faces etched with concern.

"Something's wrong," I said, my voice trembling. "Zoya's been gone for too long, and she's not answering her phone. I think Farida and Rauf might be behind it."

Riya's eyes widened. "We need to do something. This isn't right."

Azal clenched his fists, his face darkening with anger. "We can't just sit here. We need to find out the reason why she's not returning any of our calls."

As the days passed with no updates, I finally broke down and told everyone the truth about Zoya's situation. The group listened in stunned silence as I recounted her traumatic past, her stepmother's ruthlessness, and the threats she faced.

"I... I didn't know how to tell you all," I confessed, my voice wavering. "Zoya's been through so much more than any of us knew and she didn't want me to tell you. Her stepmother, Farida, and her stepbrother, Rauf, have been tormenting her ever since her father died. They've been trying to take everything from her."

Abad's face was a mask of disbelief. "All this time, we thought she was just dealing with personal stuff. We had no idea it was this bad."

Preeti's eyes were filled with tears. "How could they do this to her? She's been carrying this weight all alone."

Siddhart looked at me with a mixture of concern and anger. "We need to do something. We can't let her face this on her own."

Realizing that waiting was no longer an option, I made a decision that would alter everything. "I'm going to Lucknow. I need to see what's happening and find a way to help her."

The group tried to dissuade me, worried for my safety and unsure of what I could accomplish alone. But my mind was made up.

The group was initially hesitant. Abad, Siddhart, and Azal tried to convince me to let them come along, but I shook my head. "We can't all show up at her doorstep asking questions. I need to do this alone."

Aryan stepped forward, his expression resolute. "If you're going to fight for her, Fawaz, you'll need someone by your side. I'm coming with you."

I hesitated, but Aryan's words struck a chord. "I lost my girl because I didn't fight for her," he said quietly. "If you're going to fight for Zoya, you need someone who understands what it means to stand by your side."

I looked around at the concerned faces of our friends, and then back at Aryan. Seeing his determination, I finally agreed. "Alright, Aryan. We'll go together."

We both made excuses to our parents, explaining that we were going to Lucknow for a trip. After an hour of convincing them, our parents reluctantly agreed and called our hostel to inform them of my absence.

With our plans set, Aryan and I prepared for the journey. As we boarded the train, I could feel the weight of the mission ahead. But I was determined to find Zoya, to confront Farida and Rauf, and to do whatever it took to help her. The journey to Lucknow felt like the beginning of a fight that would test everything we had.

As the train rolled away from the station, I glanced at Aryan, who gave me a reassuring nod. Together, we were heading into a storm, but we were ready to face it.

Chapter-32

When Aryan and I finally reached Lucknow, the sun was high in the sky, casting its harsh light on the bustling streets. Our urgency led us straight to Zoya's locality, where I knew her mansion was located. Her house was located at the outskirts of the city and there was a big garden filled with trees which also looked like a forest surrounding it. As we asked around, an old man with a grizzled beard pointed us towards a grand, imposing structure at the end of the street. The gate bore the name "Himani's Mansion" in elegant script.

We approached the massive gate, our hearts pounding with a mix of fear and hope. I knocked firmly, my knuckles rapping sharply against the ornate wood. The door creaked open, revealing a disheveled man in a baniyan. His unkempt appearance made it clear that he was Rauf. The sight of him made my blood boil, and I had to fight the urge to lash out.

"Where's Zoya?" I demanded, my voice a low growl. "She's not answering her phone, and she's been missing for weeks."

Rauf's eyes were cold and dismissive. "She's not here," he said flatly, his tone devoid of any empathy.

I could see the deceit in his eyes. "Don't lie to me. I know she's here."

Rauf's expression darkened, and before I could react, he pushed me aside, slamming the door shut with a finality that echoed in my ears. Aryan quickly moved to help me up, his face a mask of grim determination. "Come on, Fawaz. Let's go."

We retreated to a nearby hotel, my mind racing with anger and frustration. The waiting was excruciating, each moment stretching into eternity as we planned our next move. When the sun began to dip below the horizon, casting long shadows across the city, we returned to the mansion.

The light from one of the upper windows caught my eye. As I focused on it, I could see three dark silhouettes moving around in the room—Farida, Rauf, and Zoya. My heart ached as I watched Zoya, her posture stiff with fear and defiance, standing between her tormentors. They seemed to be questioning her about our presence, and I could see her struggling to keep her composure.

Then, the two other figures left the room, leaving Zoya alone. Moments later, the window creaked open just a sliver, and Zoya's tear-streaked face appeared, her eyes scanning the darkness below.

When our gazes met, it was like time stood still. A tear slipped down my cheek, mirroring the one that traced its way down Zoya's face. At that moment, all I wanted was to hold her close, to take her away from this nightmare and into the safety of my arms. I fumbled for my flashlight, turning it on and off in a slow, rhythmic pattern to catch her attention.

Through the dim beam of light, I tried to convey my message. On-off, on-off—slow and deliberate. The pattern formed a question: *Are you okay?*

Zoya's eyes widened, and she responded with sign language. *I'm okay, but I'm trapped.*

Her message was clear: despite her current circumstances, she was trying to stay strong. My heart ached with the weight of helplessness and longing. I pointed to the mansion and then made a gesture as if breaking free. I wanted her to know that we were going to find a way in, that we weren't going to give up on her.

Zoya's face was a mask of both relief and fear. Her eyes seemed to say, *Please hurry. They're dangerous.*

The window began to close, and I saw Zoya's form retreat into the shadows of the room. As the window shut, I felt a surge of determination. I had to find a way to get inside, to confront Farida and Rauf, and to rescue Zoya from this nightmare.

Aryan stood beside me, his expression one of steely resolve. "We'll get her out of there, Fawaz. We just need a plan."

My hands were shaking, but I nodded, squeezing Aryan's shoulder for support. Together, we would face whatever challenges lay ahead, and we would bring Zoya back to the safety and love she deserved.

Chapter-33

The next night hung heavy with anxiety as Aryan and I crouched beneath the imposing facade of Zoya's mansion. The only sound was the whisper of the wind and the occasional distant hum of the city. I flicked my torch in a rhythmic pattern—three short flashes followed by a pause. It was our signal, a beacon of hope in the darkness. Moments later, Zoya's silhouette appeared at the window, her face illuminated by the faint light of a candle inside.

"Fawaz!" Her voice, though barely a whisper, was filled with a blend of fear and relief. "What are you doing here?"

"I came to get you out," I said, my voice firm despite the racing pulse in my chest. "There's a tree outside. It's a risk, but it's our best chance."

Zoya's eyes reflected her worry. "It's dangerous. You shouldn't have come."

"I'm not leaving without you," I insisted, my determination unshaken. "We'll make it work. Trust me."

Her gaze was a turbulent sea of fear and gratitude. "You're crazy, but I'm relieved you're here."

With a final, reassuring look, I began the climb. The tree was gnarled and its branches twisted, making the ascent a grueling test of strength and resolve. The branch leading to the window was at least two meters away, an imposing gap that seemed almost insurmountable. Every movement felt like it could be the one that ended in disaster, but my focus was unyielding. With a powerful leap, I grabbed the ledge and hoisted myself through the window.

The room was cloaked in darkness, the power cut off in the locality. The only source of light was a single candle flickering weakly on a small table. The shadows danced across the walls, creating an eerie yet intimate atmosphere.

As soon as I landed, Zoya's arms were around me, pulling me into a tight embrace. The warmth of her body contrasted sharply with the cold darkness, and her relief was palpable. Her tears soaked into my shirt, and I could feel her trembling against me.

"I was so scared," she whispered, her voice breaking. "I didn't know if you'd make it."

"I'm here now," I said softly, my heart aching with a mixture of relief and sorrow. "We're going to get out of here. We'll figure it out."

Zoya leaned on me, her breath uneven as she cried silently. Her body trembled against mine, and the weight of her sorrow pressed down on me like a suffocating blanket. Each tear that slipped down her cheek felt like a dagger to my heart, a vivid reminder of the pain and fear she had been enduring alone. I could feel her heart racing, its rhythm a frantic drumbeat that mirrored my own.

In that dark room, where shadows stretched and twisted around us like phantom limbs, we found a fleeting sliver of light in our unity. The candle's flickering flame cast an ethereal glow, illuminating our faces with a soft, trembling light that only made the darkness around us seem more profound. The oppressive silence was punctuated only by Zoya's quiet sobs and the occasional gust of wind rustling outside. It felt like the world had narrowed down to just the two of us, suspended in a moment that seemed both painfully fleeting and eternally fragile.

I gently cupped her face, my thumbs brushing away the tears that stained her cheeks. Her skin was warm, but her eyes were cold with fear. "Zoya, I'm here," I whispered, my voice trembling with the weight of my emotions. "You're not alone in this."

She looked up at me, her eyes glistening with a mixture of desperation and relief. "Fawaz… I don't know how much longer I can endure this," she said, her voice barely more than a whisper. "They've been holding me here because I refuse to sign the documents," Zoya explained through her sobs. "They want to sell my father's company. I can't let them do that. I won't. That's all I have left."

The window, three floors up, was our only option for escape. I glanced at the daunting drop, my stomach knotting with apprehension. But time was against us, and we had no choice but to take the risk. I made a quick assessment of the room, looking for anything that could assist in our escape.

As we prepared to move, the sound of footsteps echoed ominously through the hallway. Zoya's eyes widened in terror. "It's them. You have to leave now."

My heart was heavy with the thought of abandoning her, even temporarily. "I'll come back for you. Just hold on."

I climbed back to the window, my body trembling with both fear and pain. The jump was perilous, but there was no turning back. With a deep breath, I leapt, reaching for the branch below. The impact was jarring, and I felt a sharp, searing pain in my right hand as I tumbled to the ground.

I landed with a painful thud, my body crumpling awkwardly. The agony in my shoulder was intense, and I could feel the sharp stab of injury in my right hand. Through the haze of pain, I saw Rauf emerging from the mansion, his face a mask of rage.

Rauf's eyes locked onto me as he saw me on the ground. His fury erupted, and he stormed back inside. The sounds of his rage were unmistakable—Zoya's terrified screams, the resounding slap, and his harsh demands for his sister Farida. The realization that Zoya was being harmed in front of me fueled my anguish and desperation.

Aryan arrived just in time, his face etched with concern and resolve. "We have to go," he urged, his voice strained with urgency. "We can't stay here. It's too dangerous."

Reluctantly, I allowed Aryan to help me up, my injured arm hanging limply by my side. As I glanced back at the mansion, my heart ached with a mix of rage and sorrow. Zoya stood alone, her figure a beacon of resilience amidst the torment. The sight of her suffering left a deep scar on my soul.

Aryan and I fled through the darkened streets, the pain in my shoulder a constant reminder of our harrowing situation. We sought refuge in a nearby alley, where I collapsed against the cold, hard wall. Aryan crouched beside me, his eyes filled with a determined fire.

"We'll get her out of this," Aryan said firmly, despite the bleakness of our situation. "We'll find a way."

I nodded, my heart heavy with the weight of the night's events. The struggle was far from over, but with Aryan by my side, I knew we had a fighting chance.

Chapter-34

The air was thick with the tension of our impending rescue mission. Aryan and I stood in the gloom, our breaths mingling with the cold night air as we prepared for another attempt to save Zoya.

As we neared the mansion, my heart pounded with a mix of hope and dread. The window through which we had earlier escaped was now securely shut. The challenge seemed even greater than before. Aryan, his face set with grim determination, began climbing the tree. His movements were swift and practiced, but every branch he ascended felt like an eternity to me. I watched in tense silence, praying that this time would be different.

Aryan's figure finally disappeared into the darkness of the window. I could hear the sound of glass breaking—sharp and jarring in the quiet night. The minutes stretched into what felt like hours before Aryan reappeared. His face was grim, but his eyes held a fierce resolve as he motioned for Zoya to climb down.

When Zoya emerged from the window, she looked both fragile and defiant. Her eyes met mine with a mix of fear and desperation. I pulled her into a fierce embrace, our kiss desperate and filled with a poignant blend of relief and sorrow. For a fleeting moment, we were together, our love burning bright even amidst the encroaching darkness.

Aryan's voice cut through the haze of emotion. "We need to move," he said urgently. "We have to get out of here."

We hurried towards the car, the urgency of our escape palpable. The sudden burst of gunfire shattered the stillness, the sharp cracks echoing through the night. My heart raced as Aryan fell, a pained cry piercing the silence. Blood stained the ground, and I could see the agony etched on his face as he clutched his injured leg. It was Rouf.

Panic surged through me, mingling with the throbbing pain in my broken hand. With a gritted jaw and strained muscles, I lifted Aryan, each movement a struggle against my own injuries. His weight was a heavy burden, his breathing ragged and labored. The urgency of our situation was clear....every second counted, and every delay could be fatal.

Then, a heart-stopping cry from Zoya made me turn. She had collapsed, her body crumpled in a heap. The sight was like a dagger to my heart. Two more gunshots rang out, each one a grim reminder of the danger still closing in. The panic in my chest surged to new heights. I had to choose between Zoya and Aryan, and the decision felt like a knife twisting in my soul.

Aryan's voice was strained, filled with anguish and urgency. "Fawaz, we need to go now!" he shouted, his eyes reflecting the dire gravity of our situation.

I felt a wrenching sense of helplessness as I looked between Zoya's fallen form and Aryan's fading consciousness. The realization of our predicament was almost unbearable. I knew that if we stayed, we might all be lost. I had to make a choice.

With a heart full of guilt and fear, I made the agonizing decision to leave Zoya behind. My stomach churned with the weight of that choice as I started the car, the engine roaring to life with a sound that seemed to cut through the night's silence.

As we sped away, I glanced back, the sight of Zoya's anguished face fading into the distance was a haunting image that would forever scar my memory.

The car raced through the night, the road blurring beneath us as adrenaline and despair coursed through my veins. Aryan's labored breathing was a constant reminder of our peril, each breath a testament to the price of our escape. The road felt endless, each mile a harsh reminder of the loved one we had left behind.

As we finally reached safety, the crushing weight of failure settled over me. I had promised to protect Zoya, but in my desperate bid to save Aryan, I had left her to face the torment alone. The echoes of gunfire and Zoya's tear-streaked face haunted me, a relentless reminder of my broken promise.

Aryan's condition demanded immediate medical attention, but my mind was consumed by the pain of our loss. The future was shrouded in uncertainty, darkened by the shadows of our failed rescue and the daunting challenges that lay ahead. Each moment of relief was tainted by the relentless ache of regret and sorrow.

Chapter-35

The hospital's sterile lights were a stark contrast to the chaos that had enveloped my life. I stayed by Aryan's side, my every thought consumed by guilt and fear for Zoya. Each beep of the monitor and each water drip felt like a ticking clock, reminding me of the precious time slipping away. I tended to Aryan's needs with a heavy heart, knowing that every moment spent away from Zoya was another moment she could be suffering.

The hospital was a brief reprieve, but my mind was consumed by the image of Zoya alone and suffering. After ensuring Aryan was in safe hands, I returned to the mansion, determined to confront Rouf and Farida. The sight that met me was nightmarish—Zoya was bound again, bloodied, and sprawled on the floor. Her screams pierced the silence, a chilling symphony of agony.

My rage was uncontrollable. I stormed into the room, fury propelling me forward. I grabbed a nearby flower vase and brought it down on Rouf's head with all the strength I could muster. He fell, unconscious, and I continued to strike him until my hands were numb.

Farida's sudden appearance was a jolt to my senses. She pointed a gun at Zoya, her eyes cold and unfeeling. "Surrender now, or she dies," she warned, her voice devoid of sympathy. The sight of the gun aimed at Zoya brought me to my knees, my hands raised in surrender. My heart ached as I watched Zoya's cries of despair, her helplessness a reflection of my own.

Farida's command was ruthless. She bound my hands and feet with tight ropes, leaving me prostrate before Zoya. Her sobs were a haunting melody of suffering, and I could only watch in helpless agony as Farida tended to her wounds. The bandage Farida applied was a small comfort amidst the brutality, but it did little to ease the pain or the blood loss.

Days passed in a haze of pain and despair. The food offered was a cruel mockery of our situation, and my refusal to eat only drew more violence from Rouf. His brutal punch left me spitting blood, a grim testament to my helplessness.

On the third day, Aryan's call came through. The screen flashed his name, but I couldn't answer. He knew the truth, and the silence between us was a cruel reminder of our shared predicament. When Rouf reappeared, his expression was inscrutable, his intentions unknown.

He started peeling Zoya's clothes off in front of me. A wave of terror surged through my mind. She kicked him in the face, only intensifying his rage, and he responded by slapping her hard.

"Mother fucker....get off of her." I screamed at him.

"Now you're gonna have to watch what I am about to do....you dog. This is for hitting me." He replied.

Once Zoya was half naked, he forced himself into her. I was there watching all of it....screaming my heart out but couldn't do anything. He continued harassing her for 15 minutes straight and Zoya's face was now filled with a mix of pain, anger, and suffocation. Once he was done, he brought a lighter and burned her reproductive part. She screamed in pain, her voice tearing through the air like a raw, agonized cry from the depths of her soul. It was as if every ounce of suffering she had held inside was unleashed in that moment, a sound so powerful and heart-wrenching that it sent shivers down my spine. The anguish in her scream was unbearable, echoing around us.

Suddenly, a loud, jarring knock echoed through the house, ripping through the suffocating silence. The sound was like a harbinger of doom. Rouf dashed frantically into the other room, his face pale with fear. Farida's scream pierced the air, her voice cracking with desperation, "It's the police!"

They opened the back door and rushed out. Some of the policemen chased them.

Amid the chaos, two figures appeared, their presence a beacon of hope. One of them moved swiftly to cover Zoya, his actions protective and determined, while the other cut the ropes binding me with a precision that spoke of urgency and skill. As soon as I was free, I bolted towards Zoya, my heart hammering in my chest, a maelstrom of dread and hope swirling within me.

There she was, lying on the ground, her usually vibrant eyes now dulled by pain and exhaustion. The serenity in her face was unnervingly calm, but there was a distant look in her eyes that told me she was drifting in and out of consciousness. I knelt beside her, my heart shattering as I saw the bruises and the marks of her suffering.

"Zoya," I said, my voice trembling with a blend of desperation and sorrow. "We're safe now. We've made it. Please, hang on."

A single tear slid down her cheek, glistening like a drop of sorrow in the dim light. Her lips moved faintly, and her voice, though weak, held a depth of emotion that cut through the chaos. "Fawaz… My life has been a hell from the beginning, ever since I was a child. But having you in my life, even for this short time, has been a solace I didn't expect."

"No, Zoya," I begged, clutching her hand as if it were my only lifeline. "We still have time. We can be together. Please, stay with me..."

Her smile was fragile, a fleeting glimpse of beauty amidst the pain. "Thank you for every moment we shared," she said, her voice cracking. "I was destined to be trapped here, but... I love you, Fawaz." Her words were a bittersweet whisper, each one tinged with the pain of a life cut short. Tears streamed down her face, her body trembling with the intensity of her emotions.

"Zoya, don't leave me," I cried, shaking her gently, my voice breaking with anguish. "Please, wake up! I need you!"

But there was no response. I felt for her pulse, my fingers trembling with fear and hope, but there was nothing. The realization hit me with a crushing finality. Her warmth was fading, her body growing cold in my arms. My heart felt as though it was being torn apart as the reality of her loss sunk in.

Two policemen arrived with a stretcher, their expressions solemn and resigned. One of them checked her body with a clinical detachment that only deepened my grief. He looked at me with a gaze full of compassion and said softly, "She's gone."

I held Zoya close, my tears mingling with the blood and dirt on her clothes. I cradled her in my arms, feeling the weight of her lifeless form against me. The world seemed to spin around us, the edges of reality blurring as I sobbed uncontrollably. Every breath felt like a suffocating reminder of her absence.

In those final moments, all that remained was the profound sadness of our love—brief, intense, and now irrevocably lost. The memories of her laughter, her touch, and the whispered promises of a future that would never be were all that I had left. The ache in my heart was a relentless, hollow pain, a testament to the love we had shared and the life we had lost.

Chapter-36

A month had passed since the night that had shattered everything. I returned to college, my heart weighed down by a grief that refused to fade. The campus, once a place of laughter and friendship, now felt like a ghost of its former self, haunted by the absence of Zoya.

As soon as Preeti saw me, her eyes filled with the anguish that had become all too familiar. She rushed forward, her face a mask of pain, and threw her arms around me. The warmth of her embrace was both comforting and heartbreaking, her tears mingling with mine as she sobbed uncontrollably. Her grief mirrored my own, and it was a painful reminder of the loss we all shared.

One by one, the rest of our friends gathered around—Aryan, now steadier but still visibly affected by the trauma; Siddhart, whose usually bright eyes were shadowed by sorrow; Azal, who wore his melancholy like a second skin; Abad, his stoic exterior betraying the sadness within; Riya, her empathy palpable; and Sneha, her own tears a testament to the bond we had all shared with Zoya.

Each friend's presence was a quiet acknowledgment of Zoya's impact on our lives. Despite the collective sadness, I held onto a fragile thread of hope, a desperate wish that somehow Zoya might return. Yet, the reality was as harsh as it was undeniable. My friends gently pulled me back from the edge of denial, their silent support a painful reminder that Zoya was truly gone.

Back at the hostel, the familiar surroundings felt like a prison of memories. Azal and I sat on the balcony, the night air thick with the scent of grief. Azal lit a cigarette, the glow of the flame casting fleeting shadows across his face. The smoke curled upward, a wispy representation of our fleeting comfort.

I watched him for a moment, the weight of our shared sorrow heavy between us. The silence was deafening, each of us lost in our thoughts. Finally, I spoke, my voice barely above a whisper. "Light one for me too."

Azal met my gaze with a look that spoke volumes. Without a word, he handed me a cigarette. I took it, the flame briefly warming my fingers before I drew in the first, sharp breath. The smoke filled my lungs, offering a momentary escape from the relentless ache.

As I sat there, the cigarette between my fingers, my mind drifted back to that night. I had kept a piece of Zoya's clothing—a fragment of the fabric stained by the horrors she had endured. Whenever the pain became too much to bear, I would hold it close, bury my face in it, and breathe in her scent, now mingled with the bitter tang of tears and loss. Each inhalation was a painful reminder of what was lost, and I would cry uncontrollably, the fabric dampened by my tears.

The night seemed to stretch on forever, each passing moment a painful reminder of the emptiness left in Zoya's wake. The world outside continued its indifferent march, but for us, time had stalled, leaving us to grapple with the raw, jagged edges of our sorrow. In the quiet, heavy with unspoken emotions, there was a fragile solace in knowing that, even in our grief, we were not alone.